THE DRUMS OF LOVE

The lovely young Nun walked into the garden and André found that he was following her.

"It is very pretty," she said.

"And so are you."

She looked up at him in surprise, and as their eyes met, it was impossible to look away.

They just stood staring at each other. It seemed as if the whole garden vibrated like the sun itself.

"What has happened to us?" André asked and the words were almost a whisper. "I want to hold you, kiss you, yet I know it is forbidden . . ."

The Nun gave a little cry and put up her hands to cover her eyes.

"I . . . I must not . . . listen to you!"

Instinctively André reached out his arms towards her.

"Oh God!" he cried. "I cannot help myself!"

Bantam Books by Barbara Cartland
Ask your bookseller for the books you have missed

Barbara Cartland's Library of Love series

Barbara Cartland's Ancient Wisdom series

Other Books by Barbara Cartland

RECIPES FOR LOVERS

Barbara Cartland
The Drums of Love

BANTAM BOOKS · TORONTO · NEW YORK · LONDON

THE DRUMS OF LOVE
A Bantam Book / February 1979

ISBN 0-553-12572-9

Published simultaneously in the United States and Canada

Bantam Books are published by Bantam Books, Inc. Its trade-
mark, consisting of the words "Bantam Books" and the por-
trayal of a bantam, is Registered in U.S. Patent and Trademark
Office and in other countries. Marca Registrada. Bantam
Books, Inc., 666 Fifth Avenue, New York, New York 10019.

PRINTED IN THE UNITED STATES OF AMERICA

Author's Note

When I visited Haiti I met Katherine Dunham, who knows more about Voodoo than anyone else in the country.

A famous black ballerina, now retired, she has her own Voodoo Temple in the garden of her beautiful home. She gave me a meteorite thunderson, one of which is kept in every Temple and in the possession of every Priest or *Papaloi*.

I also attended the Temple belonging to Jean Beauvoir, a Doctor of Science. I saw a performance given by his Voodoo adepts, although I was not allowed to stay for a private ceremony given afterwards, which was only for the initiated. The dancing was sensational, the drums mesmeric. I have described it as truthfully as possible in this story.

Voodoo, which is now allowed by law in Haiti, concerns, I was told, over sixty percent of the population. Catholicism and Voodoo meet on what is nearly common ground.

Chapter One

1805

"We are coming in to Port!"

Kirk Horner rose as he spoke and walked to the port-hole to look out at the Harbour of Port-au-Prince, which was filled with small boats and ships, but none of them as large as the American Schooner in which he was travelling.

"Now my adventure begins!" a voice said from behind him, and the tall, square-jawed American turned to look at the speaker.

"Change your mind, André," he begged. "Come back to Boston with me. You are making a mistake which you may bitterly regret, if you remain alive to feel anything."

"We have been all through this before," André de Villaret replied, "and the alternative to living in penury for the rest of my life is, I assure you, a very efficient spur."

"It's crazy! Absolutely crazy!" Kirk Horner said positively. "But I suppose I shall have to help you, although it goes against my better instincts."

"You promised you would help me before I came on board, and I am holding you to that promise," André de Villaret replied. "So, what do we do now?"

Kirk Horner turned once again to look out the port-hole.

Beyond the Harbour lay the town of Port-au-

1

Prince, and beyond that were the mountains, purple and blue, which looked dark and menacing even in the brilliant sunshine.

Everything else was green, so deeply green that it appeared almost dazzling and seemed to make the white houses in the distance have about them a strange luminosity which would not have been apparent in any other climate.

"What I want you to do," Kirk said, "is to stay here on board until I can make contact with the one person who I think will be able to help you on this mad goose-chase."

"Who is he?" André de Villaret asked.

"His name is Jacques Dejean, and he is a Mulatto."

This, André de Villaret knew, meant a man born of one black parent and one white parent.

He had seen Mulattos in America, and Kirk had already told him that in Haiti the Mulattos despised the blacks, and the blacks hated the Mulattos almost as much as they hated the white men.

It was, as Kirk had said, a wild, unbelievably crazy adventure for a Frenchman to attempt to enter Haiti at the moment.

Jean-Jacques Dessalines, Commander-in-Chief of the Haitian Army, who had been instrumental in massacring with bestial cruelty the French planters and almost every other white person on the island, had the previous year made himself Emperor of Haiti.

One of his first actions after the Declaration of Independence was celebrated was to design new uniforms for his soldiers.

Two thousand of them had been supplied by a Boston firm, and they were at that moment aboard the Schooner in which André de Villaret and his friend Kirk Horner had sailed to Haiti.

Kirk had been commissioned to make a private report to the American President on the conditions on the island.

The Americans were intent on re-establishing themselves in the market from which the late General

Leclerc, brother-in-law of Napoleon Bonaparte, had evicted them.

However, the French Vice-Consul in Philadelphia had protested violently against the Americans not only for trading with Dessalines's Army and sending them ship-loads of arms and ammunition, but also he accused them of sending American Negroes as recruits to fight with the rebels against what remained of the French and the Spanish.

All these services were paid for in cotton, copper, timber, and even in dollars, and Dessalines's hoard of silver was considerable.

The island had been so ravaged that it was hard for other countries to understand exactly what was happening, and Kirk Horner, who had been to Haiti two years earlier, was expecting to find things very changed under the tyrannous reign of Dessalines.

It was because of this savage sadist that he feared for the life of his friend André de Villaret.

The two men had known each other for some years and Kirk Horner had stayed with André's family when he had visited England.

It had perhaps been his descriptions of Haiti that had first aroused André's interest in the island, apart from the fact that he had a personal connection in that his uncle, a wealthy planter, had been killed in the Revolution.

He had not lost his life in the first uprising of 1791 for the simple reason that the De Villaret estate was well administered and the slaves had not been treated in the same inhuman manner as they had been on many other plantations.

But Kirk had written to tell André that his uncle and his three sons had been murdered, which he had not known until his last visit to Haiti.

He had been astounded when two months ago André had turned up in Boston and asked his help in visiting the country.

"Impossible!" Kirk had said to him. "Jean-Jacques Dessalines has vowed to kill every white man that he meets. He is fanatical in his hatred of whites, and I

would not give two cents for your life once you set
foot on Haitian soil."

He had described Dessalines to his friend:

"He is not tall, and he is shaped like a gorilla.
His wide shoulders support a thick, bull-like neck. His
thick lips curve under enormously wide nostrils and a
misshapen nose. His forehead is low and recedes to a
cap of wiry hair which nearly meets his eye-brows."

"He certainly does not sound very attractive!"
André had said, laughing.

"It is no laughing matter," Kirk said sharply. "He
strikes terror into his own people and has periods of
hysteria when he suspects everyone and talks inter-
minably of blood and destruction."

"I have heard," André said, "that he behaved in a
diabolical way, promising the white inhabitants protection if they gave themselves up, then killing them
when they trusted him."

"The streets in Jérémie ran with blood when he
murdered four hundred fifty men, women, and children," Kirk replied. "Even Christophe, his Commander-in-Chief, was appalled at his savagery!"

He paused to let what he had said sink in, then
added:

"Are you surprised that the American President
was anxious when he learnt that in drawing up the
Act of Independence, one of Dessalines's committee,
amidst wild applause, shouted:

"'To set out this Declaration we need the skin
of a white man for the parchment, his skull as an
ink-horn, his blood for ink, and a bayonet for a pen.'"

"You are making my flesh creep," André remarked.
"At the same time, I am still determined to see if I
can find the treasure that my uncle buried on his
plantation."

That was the sole object, Kirk knew, of his friend's
journey.

He had already learnt that now that André's father was dead, André himself had become the *Comte*
de Villaret and head of the family.

It was a position which he had never expected to
hold.

His grandfather had had three sons, André's father being the youngest.

Knowing that things were not going smoothly in France and that dissatisfaction was growing amongst the peasants, the second son, Philippe, had settled in Haiti early in the 1770s, deciding to make his life there.

He wrote home frequently, telling his relatives that he was becoming a very rich man, since the cotton and coffee he grew fetched good prices in every part of the New World.

Then had come the French Revolution, and the *Comte* de Villaret and his only son were amongst those taken to the guillotine.

This meant that Philippe de Villaret, in Haiti, became the head of the family, while his younger brother, François, with his English-born wife and son André, escaped as emigrés to England.

André had been brought up in English schools and had attended an English University, and most of his friends were English.

But his father had very little money and it was only through the kindness of his mother's relatives that they were able to live in any sort of comfort.

The news from Kirk that Philippe de Villaret had been murdered made André's father the head of the family, and when he died in 1803, André himself became the *Comte* de Villaret, but without any resources to support such an ancient and honoured title.

It was then that he very carefully scrutinised his Uncle Philippe's last letters from Haiti.

The last one, which must have been written only a few months before he was massacred, seemed to André very significant.

He had written to his brother:

> *Things are getting very frightening out here. Every day I hear of terrible atrocities taking place on the plantations of my friends. Men not only lose their lives but they are tortured and butchered while the women are raped or else sent to work as slaves on the plantations*

> *that are now being run by the blacks themselves.*
>   *We make plans to escape, then tear them*
> *up as we find that each idea is useless and that*
> *by drawing attention to ourselves we may pre-*
> *cipitate the fate which seems to be encroaching*
> *nearer and nearer.*

Then came the most significant sentence, which
André read over and over again:

> *I can only put my trust in the earth itself,*
> *and of course under the protection and the*
> *shadow of God.*

"That," André said to Kirk when he showed him
the letter, "is, I believe, a perfectly clear message to
my father that Uncle Philippe buried his money in the
ground somewhere near a Church."

"It certainly might be," Kirk agreed. "All the
planters buried their money and any other valuables
they possessed. Dessalines is well aware of it and has
either tortured them into revealing what they have
hidden, or else has searched so thoroughly that he now
has, I am told, an enormous amount of booty taken
from the plantations."

He paused before he added:

"When Dessalines left Jérémie, he was followed
by twenty-five mules loaded with plate and other
valuables. But I hear it did not equal what he collected in Aux Cayes, the greater part of which was
found buried underground."

"I have to take a chance on it," André said.
"After all, I was always an optimist."

"An optimist who will die," Kirk snapped, "as
thousands of your countrymen have died already."

Then he smiled.

"One piece of luck is that you do not look French.
You are too big."

"You have forgotten that my mother was English,"
André said.

There was no doubt, his friend thought, that the
Comtesse de Villaret had transmitted to her son the
characteristics of the men in her family.

André had the dark hair and dark eyes of his father, but he had the height which was characteristic of his mother's family.

Broad shoulders, narrow hips, and an athletic figure were regarded as the right image for the elegant Bucks who surrounded the Prince of Wales in London.

André was also quite formidably strong, but that, Kirk thought despondently, was not likely to save him in Haiti when he had a white skin.

He turned to stare once again out the port-hole and said:

"With any luck my friend Jacques Dejean will come aboard when he sees our ship arrive. He has been expecting me, or should have been, for the last two months."

"You have friends everywhere," André said good-humouredly.

"One needs them in the world in which I work," Kirk replied.

"What you are really saying is that you need spies to ferret out what is going on," André retorted. "But I do not care what your friends are like, or who they are, as long as they will help me."

"You are insufferably self-centred!" Kirk said, laughing.

But he thought it was typical of his friend to concentrate, to the exclusion of all else, on what he had decided to do.

Kirk left the cabin, and André sat with a look on his face which his family would have known meant that he was determined to the point of obstinacy.

He not only had to fight against his mother's pleading not to come on this expedition, and to argue every minute of the day with Kirk, but he was also, because he was a realist, well aware of the odds against which he was pitting himself.

The whole story of the revolution of the slaves in Haiti, the burning of the town of Le Cap when General Leclerc tried to land, the death of Leclerc himself of yellow fever, and the renewal of the war between France and Britain, was one of disaster for the French.

But from what André had heard about the treatment by the French planters of their slaves, the rebellion might have been expected to take place sooner or later.

The slaves themselves had been fortunate in having two extremely brilliant Leaders in Jean-Jacques Dessalines and Henri Christophe.

Dessalines might be a brute and a sadist but he was also a brave and experienced soldier. Christophe, who was much the kinder and more reasonable of the two men, had pleaded successfully for the lives of some of the Frenchmen who dealt honestly with the blacks and those—notably Priests and Surgeons—who had served with them.

Nevertheless, as André knew, nine-tenths of the French population had perished and Dessalines was still killing and torturing those whom he found alive.

André drew a deep breath.

"If I die—I die!" he said to himself. "At the same time, it is worth the risk, and at least my blood will mingle with that of my compatriots, which already stains the soil of Haiti."

The door of the cabin opened and Kirk reappeared.

"Good news!" he exclaimed. "I was right in thinking that Jacques Dejean would be expecting me. He has already come aboard, and now you can meet him."

He was followed into the cabin by a man whom André looked at sharply, knowing that so much depended on him.

Jacques Dejean's skin was a golden brown, and if André had seen him in England he might merely have thought he was sun-tanned. However, while his features were European, there was a suspicious curl in his black hair and his eyes were very dark.

He was as elegantly dressed as Kirk and André, his crisp muslin cravat tied with unmistakable elegance, and his coat, which was a somewhat flashy blue, fitted him almost too perfectly.

"Jacques," Kirk said, "this is my friend André, who needs your help, and I have told him that you will not refuse him any assistance that you can give."

"Any friend of yours...!" the Mulatto replied.
"You know that I have vowed myself to your service."

His exaggerated manner of speech in fact rang
true, and André, looking at him, thought that he was
a man to be trusted.

However, he looked at his friend Kirk to be quite
certain that he could trust the newcomer, and as if he
understood what André asked without words, Kirk
said:

"Once, in a very rough sea, I saved Jacques's life.
He has always promised to help me in return, and that
includes you. He never breaks his promises."

"That is true," Jacques said. "And so, *Monsieur*,
what can I do for you?"

Both André and Kirk looked startled. To be ad-
dressed as *"Monsieur"* made it quite clear that
Jacques, without being told, knew that he was speaking to a Frenchman.

Kirk walked to the cabin door to make quite certain that it was tightly closed. Then he asked:

"Is my friend's nationality so obvious?"

"I am a student of mankind," the Mulatto replied, "and the very fact that he wants my help and
would not come out on deck to meet me makes me
suspicious. When I saw him I was quite certain he was
not an American."

André laughed.

"I had intended to say I was English, the nation
from which half of my blood is derived."

"Half my blood is white," Jacques replied, "but
the whites have never accepted me, except when I am
useful to them."

He did not speak bitterly, he just stated a fact.

"Very well, I admit I am French. My name, which
Kirk omitted to mention, is André de Villaret."

The Mulatto thought for a moment, then he said:

"You are a relation of the De Villaret whose plantation was in the valley of the Black Mountains?"

"That is right."

"He is dead."

"That is what Kirk told me two years ago."

"Then why are you here?" Jacques asked inquisitively.

André decided to tell the truth, feeling he had nothing to lose.

"I believe my uncle buried money and other treasures somewhere on his estate. As his sons died with him and I am now head of the family, that money belongs to me."

"You will be fortunate if our noble Emperor has left it for you," Jacques replied.

"Is there any way we could find out whether or not he has discovered it?" André asked. "And if he has not, I want to go to the De Villaret plantation."

Jacques Dejean threw out his hands.

"You want!" he exclaimed. "But it is not easy. Believe me, it is very difficult to do either of those things."

"Come on, Jacques," Kirk interposed. "You know as well as I do that if anyone can help André, you are the man. There must be some way of discovering what Dessalines has pilfered and from whom. I have heard he has enormous stores of loot stacked away in the mountains."

"That is true," Jacques agreed, "but he cannot write, he does not keep accounts, and I doubt if he trusts anyone else with an inventory of his spoils."

André gave a shrug of his shoulders, as if he felt that this was a blind alley which would get them nowhere.

Then Jacques said:

"There is one person who might know whether Dessalines's treasure-house includes anything from the De Villaret plantation."

"Who is that?" Kirk asked.

"Orchis!" he replied briefly.

"Orchis!" Kirk exclaimed. "Is she here in Port-au-Prince?"

Jacques nodded.

"She has set herself up in the Habitation Leclerc and models herself on Napoleon Bonaparte's sister, who lived there when married to General Leclerc and who after his death returned to Europe and is now Her Imperial Highness Paulina Borghese."

"I can hardly believe it!" Kirk exclaimed.

"Who is this Orchis?" André asked.

Kirk laughed.

"If you stay in Haiti for long, you will soon hear of Orchis!"

"Who is she?" André asked again.

"She is one of Dessalines's mistresses," Kirk explained. "He has twenty of them, but she is better at her profession than most of the others. Although they all enjoy a regular and handsome allowance from the Imperial Purse, it is suspected that Orchis has stolen the purse itself!"

Jacques burst out laughing.

"That is an excellent description, my friend!" he remarked. "But the extravagance of Orchis has exceeded all bounds in the last year or so. Now she would like to have herself crowned Empress, but unfortunately Dessalines already has a wife!"

He laughed again before he said:

"However, she makes up for her lack of respectability by playing the part of the Princess Paulina with a brilliance that is quite indescribable."

"You say she has moved into the Habitation Leclerc?" Kirk asked.

"She receives her suitors at breakfast-time and in the evening. That is when *Monsieur* de Villaret must meet her."

"I should have thought that was impossible," Kirk remarked.

"As himself—certainly!" Jacques answered. "But if he intends to leave Port-au-Prince for the country, he must not in any circumstances step ashore as a white man."

Both André and Kirk looked astonished and Jacques explained:

"There are still a few white men here in the Port. Some are American armourers and munitions workers, but even they are hardly tolerated by Dessalines. For

a white man to go outside the town would invite
death within the first few miles."

"Then what are you suggesting?" Kirk asked.

Jacques looked at André and seemed to inspect
him from head to foot.

"You will make a very handsome Mulatto!"

"A Mulatto!" André exclaimed.

"Fortunately your hair is dark," Jacques said,
"though we may have to curl it a little. If your eyes
had been blue or grey, my task might have been more
difficult, but they are dark enough, *Monsieur*, to pass
muster, with your skin the same colour as mine."

"I must say I never thought of disguising myself,"
André said a little ruefully.

"Then you will die!" Jacques exclaimed. "And if
Dessalines or his followers have anything to do with it,
I promise you it will not be a pleasant experience!"

"No, I understand that," André said quickly.

He remembered the atrocities that had been per-
petrated not only on Frenchmen but also on some of
the Mulattos.

He also recalled that Dessalines had once ordered a man to be brought to his room, and while in
conversation he stabbed him through his heart with
his poniard.

Jacques Dejean was right, he thought. He must
disguise himself, for no-one in Haiti must suspect for
a moment that he was a white man, and French at
that.

"I will go home now," Jacques said, "and return
with a dye which comes from the bark of a certain
tree and is exactly what you need to disguise the
colour of your skin. Also, *Monsieur*, if I may suggest it,
find your most elaborate and conspicuous clothes. We
Mulattos like to flaunt ourselves!"

He turned to the door and as he reached it asked:

"Do you know any Creole?"

"I have been learning it for the last year," André
replied, "mostly, I admit, from books, but there is a
Creole aboard this ship who has been giving me les-
sons."

"That is good," Jacques said. "Mulattos are often, as Kirk will tell you, extremely well educated. I have diplomas to prove my cleverness, but I find that my head is more reliable."

André was laughing as Jacques went from the cabin. Then he settled down to wait patiently for his return.

* * *

It was nearly evening and the sun was sinking behind the mountains when two Mulattos were rowed ashore from the American Schooner.

André had been painted all over with a dye which, he had found when Jacques brought it to him, smelt abominably.

"That stinks!" he remarked, looking at the bowl in the Mulatto's hand and the sponge with which he intended to apply it.

"Once on the body, the smell will go off," Jacques replied. "But you need not only a brown skin for this deception, you must also change your way of thinking."

For the first time there was a bitterness in Jacques's voice as he went on:

"Mulattos have been continually snubbed by the whites, which has finally driven us, unwillingly, to the side of the Negroes."

"I had heard that," André said.

"We have never been liked or trusted by the blacks," Jacques went on, "but because we have superior education and in many cases the white man's abilities, we have risen to positions of importance and they have found us useful. At the same time, we live in a No-Man's-Land between black and white, and it is not a happy position."

"I understand," André said, "and therefore I am all the more grateful to you for helping me."

By the time he was covered all over with the brown dye, the smell had evaporated, and he stared at himself in the mirror critically.

There was no doubt that it altered his appear-

ance. He had seen men as sun-tanned as he appeared
now, and he wondered if anyone would actually be
deceived.

As if Jacques knew what he was thinking, he said:

"Think yourself into the part. You are a Mulatto—
always a little unsure of yourself and a little on the
defensive."

He smiled as he added:

"It is what the Americans call a 'chip on the
shoulder.' It is what all Mulattos are born with."

"And where do I come from? What is my history?"

"You belong to Haiti but have been educated in
America," Jacques replied. "Your name is André—no
point in changing that, and I think too that you might
say that you are a De Villaret. After all, as your father
was a white man, you would take his name, not your
mother's."

"Are you suggesting that I say my father was
Philippe de Villaret, who was actually my uncle?"
André asked.

"Why not?" Jacques enquired. "Then if you ask
questions about the De Villaret estate, everyone will
understand, and they will also know that because you
are a Mulatto, you are not a claimant."

"That is clever," Kirk said. He had come into the
room while André was finishing dressing.

"Very clever!" André agreed. "Thank you,
Jacques."

"All you have to prove now is whether you can
get away with it," Jacques said, "and that is up to
you."

"What am I to do now?" André enquired.

"We go ashore. You say you have been in America
and have just returned. That will entitle you to ask
lots of questions as to what has happened while you
have been away."

He paused for a moment, then he said:

"You have not met Orchis before, but you have
heard of her. She has been predominant in Port-au-
Prince only since she moved into the Habitation Leclerc."

"Did Dessalines install her there?" Kirk asked.

"I think she installed herself," Jacques replied. "She is determined to be a grand lady. If her Voodoo works, *Madame* Dessalines may have an untimely decease, in which case Orchis will step onto the throne. At least, so she thinks."

"Is Dessalines really infatuated with her?" Kirk asked.

"He likes women who are educated, sophisticated, and experienced, and Orchis is all those things! What is more, she has all the gods working for her, and they can be very powerful."

"Are you talking about Voodoo?" André asked.

"What else?" Jacques replied.

"But I thought it was forbidden."

"It is! Both Dessalines and Christophe have outlawed it. They say it smacks of servitude and is the religion of slaves."

"But it still continues?"

"Of course it still continues!" Jacques replied. "Voodoo is part of every black man and everybody else who lives in Haiti. They could not be without it, and it is so linked in the minds of those who are Catholic that it is difficult to know where Voodoo ends and Catholicism begins."

"You astonish me!" André exclaimed.

"You will learn," Jacques replied. "And now let us call on *Madame* Orchis, and you will see what a snake looks like when it has a pretty face."

André said good-bye to Kirk and went ashore with an irrepressible sense of excitement.

This was where the big adventure began. This was where he felt that he pitted his wits against a tyrant and all those who followed him.

He had been thankful to learn from Jacques that Dessalines was in fact absent, as he was leading a military attack on the Spanish-owned part of the island.

"Will he win?" Kirk had asked when Jacques told him where the Emperor was.

"I doubt it," Jacques replied. "The Spaniards are very firmly entrenched and are good fighters."

"And if he fails?" Kirk enquired.

"Then doubtless he will try again, with more American arms and better cannon. He may then succeed."

While they were on board ship, Jacques had been very free in what he said and not afraid of showing his contempt for the newly crowned Emperor, but as soon as they stepped ashore, André sensed that he was on his guard.

They took a carriage from the Quay-side, and although it was doubtful if the coachman could overhear their conversation, Jacques deliberately talked of trivial matters as they drove through the narrow streets with their wooden houses.

They stopped at his house to leave André's luggage. It was quite an impressive structure, the wooden walls painted green.

"Port-au-Prince is getting fashionable," he said, "but, as everybody is afraid of a new assault from the French, they are not expending their money on anything that might be destroyed by cannon or fire."

André knew that he was referring once again to the fact that Christophe had set the whole of Le Cap, the Port on the other side of the island, ablaze when the French Fleet was sighted.

General Leclerc had landed to find the whole place in ruins, everything scorched and blackened. It was said that his wife, Paulina Bonaparte, had wept at the sight.

She had, however, consoled herself with a very fine house in Port-au-Prince, the Habitation Leclerc, in which Orchis was now living.

When the carriage in which they were travelling passed through the impressive iron gates, there was first a drive with thick tropical vegetation on both sides of it, and then in front of them André saw a grey stone building with a pillared doorway.

He could visualise that in the past there had been smart French sentries in their white and red uniforms to spring to attention.

Now there were only Mulattos in an elaborate crimson livery to welcome them politely and lead them through narrow passages open at the sides to *Madame*'s apartments.

Jacques whispered that just as Paulina had found the Mulattos far more handsome and infinitely more interesting than even the most dashing French Officers, Orchis also had Mulatto servants.

Paulina's Mulatto footmen had worn a tight-fitting livery that had been specially designed by *Madame* Leclerc herself to make their male charms extremely obvious.

André saw that Orchis had followed her idol's example.

They went down several steps, then under a Grecian portico supported by Ionic pillars, and found themselves walking along the side of an octagonal pool into which gushed a stream of crystal-clear water.

There were shrubs and high trees. Then two carved wooden doors were opened and they were ceremoniously ushered by the Mulatto footmen into Orchis's presence.

The room, again supported by pillars, and with unglazed windows open to the moist, warm air, was divided in two.

At the end, on a dais raised two feet above the floor, was an enormous bed shaped like a swan and piled high with frothy pillows of satin and lace.

Orchis, sitting up in bed and wearing a peignoir of pale yellow chiffon, transparent enough to reveal her purple-tipped breasts, was holding Court *à la Reine*.

Near the bed, on the lower floor, where the furniture consisted of heavy Napoleonic polished mahogany with ormolu mountings, was a crowd of nearly a dozen men.

They were mostly black, although there were several Mulattos, the majority wearing the elaborate gold-braided uniform of the Emperor's Army.

They were all obviously subserviently attentive to the woman on the bed, pushing one another out of the way to get nearer to her, attempting to attract her attention, and staring at her with wide-eyed admiration.

As if she was pleased at the advent of newcomers to her circle, Orchis called out Jacques's name after he was announced and held out her hand.

He walked to the bed-side, followed by André, and now the latter could see her at close quarters.

She was not in the least what he had expected, and she was in fact as exotic and unusual as her name.

Never had he imagined that anyone could look so beautiful and at the same time so evil.

Her bare arms, her face, and the very revealing glimpses of her body were soft gold with faintly mauve shadings. Her full red lips were passionate, provocative, and at the same time secretive.

Her green eyes seemed full of mystery but demanding and possessive. When they looked at a man, they seemed to search deep into his heart and hold him captive.

Everything about her was seductive and as sensuous as a snake. She was feline—she was as primitive as a wild animal in the jungle and as tempting as Lilith must have been in the Garden of Eden.

"Jacques!" she cried, in a caressing manner that seemed to vibrate down a man's spinal cord. "Why have you been so long in coming to see me?"

"I have been at Le Cap," Jacques explained. "But now I have returned to bring you someone whom you have never met before, and who can tell you all the latest news from America."

"America!"

Her eyes were on André, and he felt as they flickered over him as if she undressed him and he stood naked in front of her.

She was obviously pleased by what she saw, and she gave him her hand, saying:

"You must tell me what are the latest fashions and how many new millionaires there are to the millimetre in that prosperous country."

"There is a great deal I would like to tell you," André replied.

Orchis looked at him from under her eye-lashes as if she was sizing him up. Then suddenly she clapped her hands and with the air of a Queen said:

"Go—all of you! I have friends with whom I have things to discuss, and I cannot hear what they are saying for the noise you are making. Leave!"

"How can you be so cruel, *Madame?*" asked an Officer who wore such huge gold epaulettes that they made his shoulders look as broad as he was high.

"Am I ever cruel to you, Réné?" Orchis asked him. "Come tomorrow, and perhaps we will talk alone."

There was no doubt what she meant by the invitation, and it was obvious that René, whoever he might be, was appeased by the honour.

He kissed her fingers, and then the whole company, as if they knew they dare not disobey her command, left the room, leaving Orchis alone with Jacques and André.

"Sit down, *mes braves,*" she said. "There is wine if you require it."

"You go to our heads, Orchis, without any need for wine," Jacques answered gallantly.

"You were always a flatterer, and quite an insincere one," Orchis replied. "What have you done with that little *poule* who supplanted me in your affections?"

"No-one has ever done that," Jacques protested. "While I have been away she has found another protector—a General—and who can compete with that?"

He spoke in a way which made Orchis laugh from sheer amusement.

"So you have been *trompé.* Well, our Army must have some encouragement!"

She looked at André and asked:

"You do not think it is a good idea to wear the uniform of our brave Haitian soldiers?"

"I am a businessman," André said firmly.

"And talking of uniforms," Jacques interjected, "André has just arrived from America with the two thousand which the Emperor designed himself."

"They are here!" Orchis cried. "Jean-Jacques will be delighted! I only wish he could have had them in time for his victory against the Spaniards."

"A battle never improves the appearance of a

good uniform," Jacques said. "Better to keep them in readiness for the celebrations."

"Of course!" Orchis replied. "And I only hope that the Emperor's uniforms are as impressive as he hopes they will be. Otherwise, heads will undoubtedly roll!"

Jacques held up his hands.

"Not mine!" he said. "I had nothing to do with it. And my friend André de Villaret merely happened to travel with the consignment."

Orchis tilted her head to one side and said:

"I seem to know that name."

"It was quite well known before the Revolution."

"You mean there was a De Villaret of importance in Haiti?"

"One of the most prosperous plantations was owned by André's father."

"Of course! That is why I have heard the name," Orchis cried. "Well, I imagine he has no wish to work in the De Villaret cotton-fields, or whatever they grew!"

"No indeed!" André replied.

He thought that Jacques was speaking too soon of the plantation, and therefore he deliberately changed the subject of the conversation.

"You are very beautiful, *Madame*," he said. "I had heard of your charms before I went to America, and even in Boston they were talking about you. Now I find that words were very inadequate to express your beauty."

Orchis made a little sensuous movement towards him, and just for a moment her hand touched his. It was like a flicker from the tongue of a snake against his skin.

Then once again she was appraising him through narrowed eyes in a manner which made him feel he was wearing one of the tight, revealing uniforms of the Mulatto servants.

"You shall dine with me," she said at length. "I promised a certain Officer that I would be alone to-night, but I have changed my mind."

She held out her hand to Jacques.

"Tell the servants as you leave, dear Jacques, that I am not to be disturbed—not by anyone!"

"I will certainly carry your message to the front door," Jacques replied, "and I only hope I do not encounter your rejected guest with a sword in his hand."

"You will survive as you always have," Orchis replied. "As we both know, you have made yourself indispensable."

Jacques kissed her fingers and moved towards the door.

"You are a very fortunate man, André," he said as he reached it.

"I can hardly believe my good luck," André replied.

The door shut behind Jacques and Orchis turned towards André. Because he knew it was expected of him, he sat down on the side of the bed, facing her.

"You are very handsome, *mon ami*," she said. "But are you as much a man as you appear to be?"

"I can only hope so," André replied, "because, most beautiful and exotic orchid, you are very much a woman."

He felt her hands fluttering over him. Then because it was impossible not to be intrigued by her, by the invitation on her lips, by the temptation in her eyes, he bent forward.

Her lips fastened on his and he felt her sharp finger-nails digging into his back through the thin material of his coat.

He looked down into her eyes and saw himself swimming far down into their depths. He thought somewhere in the darkness there was liquid fire, and yet the fire was also within himself.

Then fireworks were exploding in his head and it was impossible to think.

Chapter Two

The first fingers of dawn were driving away the last stars of the night when André walked slowly down the drive of the Habitation Leclerc.

He had risen while Orchis was still asleep, and dressed himself with fingers that were stiff, feeling as he did so that his legs hardly belonged to him.

Never in his whole life had he known a night like the one he had spent with this woman, who seemed, even when she was asleep, to send palpable vibrations into the air round her.

They had dined under the stars in the garden outside the formal Dining-Room, which was lit by huge chandeliers and which had walls that were open on two sides.

There had only been the sound of the water falling from a fountain near them and the croak of the frogs in the tropical vegetation, which seemed to encroach upon the garden and even upon the house itself.

There had been wines to supplement delicious Creole dishes, and then Orchis had insisted on André sampling what later he knew was a "Devil's brew."

It appeared to be a liqueur with a strange fragrance about it and a taste that was different from anything he had ever drunk before.

After he had finished his glass he felt it burning through his body, running like a molten stream through every nerve and sinew, until his brain no longer seemed to function and he could only desire

Orchis in a way that he knew was unnatural and yet was irresistible.

Hours later, when they lay exhausted in the swan-shaped bed, he forced himself to remember why he was there, and said:

"I would like to hang emeralds round your neck to match your eyes, and put rubies in your ears, as red and fiery as your lips, but alas, I have no money."

"Money is not so important as that a man should be a man," Orchis answered, "and that is what you undoubtedly are, *mon cher*."

"Do you think," André asked, choosing his words with care, "that there is any money or treasure left on the De Villaret plantation?"

"What you are asking," Orchis replied, "is whether the Emperor has milked that plantation as he has milked all the others."

She laughed, and it was not a particularly pleasant sound.

"He is cunning, my Jean-Jacques. He finds all the little places, the secret caches where the whites hid their treasures, thinking they would return for them. But, as the Emperor says, there will be plenty of gold for them in the next world. They have no use for any in this."

"I could certainly do with some," André said, "if only to lay some tribute at your feet."

"There is another gift which I would much prefer at this moment," Orchis replied.

She turned towards him and her lips and hands re-ignited the fire which André thought had already burnt itself out. . . .

*   *   *

Later he tried again.

"Help me," he said, "to find what is ethically if not lawfully mine. Why should not my father pay for his pleasure, even though he would certainly not acknowledge me as his son?"

Orchis made an expression of disgust.

"*Les blancs* are always the same, *les sales cochons*," she complained. "It is right that we should

be purged of them and that those who are still left
should be punished by what is worse than death."

She spoke with a violence which André was certain she imitated from Dessalines, but somehow it was
unpleasant to hear a woman declaiming in such a
fashion and obviously enjoying the thought of those
who had died in agony.

It was all on a par with the Emperor's personal
blood-lust. But he told himself that he must be careful
to sound sympathetic, to sound as if he wanted the
death of the whites as much as those in power enjoyed their victories over their previous masters.

"Help me," he pleaded, "with my particular revenge against the man who treated my mother as a
chattel and who fathered me, neither black nor
white, into a hard and difficult world."

"He certainly equipped you with an excellent
weapon with which to ingratiate yourself!" Orchis
teased.

She ran her fingers over him before she added:

"I have a good memory, and the Emperor has always confided in me, but I cannot remember his
counting any particular plunder which came from the
De Villaret plantation. If he found anything, it was
not of importance."

This was what André wished to know, but he
was wise enough to say:

"May my father burn in Hell for having left me
with no inheritance except that of my brains."

"He also gave you—your body," Orchis said ca-
ressingly.

Then it was impossible to talk any more. . . .

*   *   *

When he had risen to leave, being careful not to
awaken the woman lying beside him, André had
looked down at her and felt a sudden revulsion that
he could not explain.

Even asleep she was breathtakingly beautiful and
lay with the grace that still had the sinuosity of a
snake.

Yet he felt himself shudder as he remembered

how she had inflamed him through the night and how, excited by the drink she had given him, he had become as much of an animal as she was herself.

As he walked down the drive, the moist air on his face was not cold enough to revive him as he would have wished.

He longed suddenly for the sharpness of an English winter with the wind blowing from the north and the intense cold of a frost.

Outside the iron gates he saw a hackney-carriage drawn by a tired horse that appeared to be asleep, as was the driver, who was curled up on the back seat.

André awakened him. The man sat up, grinning, and asked in Creole:

"Where to, *M'sieur*?"

"You wait here every night?" André enquired.

The Negro grinned again.

"Always fine gentlemen from Habitation Leclerc too tired walk."

André got into the carriage and they drove off down the hill which led towards the town.

A servant let him into Jacques Dejean's house, where both he and Kirk were staying.

He was so tired that as he climbed up the wooden staircase to his room on the first floor, he felt as if he would never reach the bed that was waiting for him.

When he got there he pulled off his boots and, without undressing further, flung himself down.

He was asleep as soon as his head touched the pillow.

* * *

It was noon when Kirk came into the room and woke him.

"Good-morning, Romeo!" he said. "You do not look as ardent this morning as you did last night."

André groaned.

"I was envying you when you set off to meet the delectable Orchis," Kirk went on, "but now I am not so sure that playing the Old Maid with Jacques was not preferable."

André sat up on the bed.

"Order me some coffee," he said, "and for God's sake stop being so humorous at this hour of the morning."

Kirk laughed and threw himself down in a comfortable chair beside a window which opened onto the balcony.

"As you are in that sort of mood," he said, "I will not tease you by asking what happened. It is very obvious from the lines under your eyes."

André groaned again and refused to talk until a servant brought him coffee and French croissants warm from the oven.

"I want a bath," he said when he had drunk the whole cup of coffee and eaten a little of the croissants.

"The servant will arrange it," Kirk answered, "but you will find it not quite up to the American style."

"I want to feel clean, and that applies to my mind as well as to my body."

"Your hangover, if that is the right word for it, will soon disperse with a little exercise," Kirk said with a smile, "and that is what Jacques has already arranged for you."

André looked at him questioningly and Kirk went on:

"You are leaving today, and I think Jacques is right. It would be a mistake for you to hang about here for too long. Although you look like a Mulatto, it might be possible for others of the same breed to penetrate your disguise."

"I was afraid of that too," André replied. "There were Mulattos in Orchis's bed-room last night, but fortunately when she was there they did not look too closely at me."

"You certainly look the part superficially," Kirk said. "But Jacques was telling me last night how important it is for you to think as a Mulatto, and that, as you well know, will not be easy."

"I shall try," André said. "There is too much at stake not to take every possible precaution. Should I come in contact with Dessalines, I am well aware what the slightest slip would mean."

"You have discovered that your uncle's treasure is still on the plantation?" Kirk questioned.

"I think so. Dessalines has never mentioned to Orchis that he has taken anything in particular from that plantation, and I gathered she follows closely what he acquires and actually has her hand in the spoils."

"Jacques says he is certain that she has an enormous amount of money and jewels stashed away," Kirk said. "Did you find out anything else of any importance?"

"There was not much time for conversation!" André said drily. "Except at dinner, when I told her a few things about America, in which she was not really interested."

It was after André had bathed, in somewhat primitive but quite effective conditions, and was dressing himself in clean clothes that Jacques returned to the house.

"I have made arrangements for you to leave Port-au-Prince this afternoon," he said, "unless, of course, Orchis has told you that such a journey is completely hopeless."

"Orchis said that Dessalines has never mentioned the De Villaret plantation or anything he acquired from there," André replied. "She was certain that that meant he had found nothing of any consequence."

"I told you that Orchis was astute," Jacques said. "If your uncle was a rich man and your aunt had valuable jewels, she would doubtless have remembered it."

"Then I must try to find the treasure myself," André said.

"But first you must do something which is very necessary unless you are to be prevented from going more than a few miles outside the town."

André looked at him apprehensively.

"What do you mean?" he asked.

"You must write a letter of glowing thanks to Orchis and send her a vast bouquet of flowers," Jacques replied.

André looked embarrassed.

"That is something I should have thought of myself."

"Paulina Leclerc was always surrounded by flowers and had more bouquets every day than the servants knew what to do with," Jacques said. "What Paulina received, Orchis expects. Write a letter with an eloquence which should come easy to a Frenchman if not to a Mulatto. But do not sign it."

André looked surprised, and Jacques explained:

"Orchis taunts Dessalines with her conquests so as to make him jealous. If she succeeds in making him think you are exceptional or a better lover than he is himself, he will inevitably remove you from the face of the earth!"

"I must admit that so far I have found Haiti a very dangerous place in which to live!" André said ruefully.

Kirk, who was listening, laughed. Then he said:

"Change your mind. Go aboard the Schooner and wait for me so that we can return to Boston together."

"I have no intention of doing anything of the sort!" André answered. "At the same time, I would like to think I have an escape route, so that when I wish to leave Haiti there will be a ship to carry me."

"There are two alternatives," Jacques said, before Kirk could speak. "First, to return here to Port-au-Prince, which, if you have found the treasure, will undoubtedly be a quite unnecessary risk. Not only Dessalines but quite a number of other people, including Christophe, will do everything possible to prevent you from taking away anything which they consider belongs to them."

André knew that this was common sense.

"If you find anything that is worthwhile," Jacques continued, "your only chance is to go to LeCap. The distance there from your uncle's plantation is about the same as coming back here."

"You think there might be an American ship at Le Cap?"

"There could easily be. Quite a lot of the cannon and ammunition that is being brought to Haiti is dis-

embarked there, and there is always a chance too of
finding your way to an English ship."

"English?" André questioned.

"The British Navy are patrolling the seas from
Jamaica up through the Windward Passage and out
into the Atlantic. That is why the Emperor knows he is
safe at the moment from a French invasion by sea."

"Of course!" André exclaimed. "And now I understand why Dessalines has attacked the Spanish part
of the island."

"There are several thousand white and coloured
troops there," Jacques replied, "and Christophe has
advanced from Le Cap along the north coast to assist
him. So your way at the moment is clear, both from
here to your uncle's plantation and then from there to
Le Cap."

"I cannot thank you enough for all your help."

"I have a horse waiting for you," Jacques continued, "and a servant to accompany you."

André looked surprised, and Jacques explained:

"You will need someone who knows the country.
You will also need a man who can talk the dialect of
the people from whom you must procure your food."

"I feel I am imposing a great deal upon you,"
André said in a low voice.

"The man I have chosen to accompany you is
someone rather special, and you can trust him as you
can trust me. His name is Tomás, and although he has
suffered the cruelty of a French master, he deprecates
as I do the cruelty of the tyrant who now rules us."

When soon after a light meal André said he was
ready to leave, he gave Jacques the letter to Orchis,
which he had composed with some care and a great
deal of imagination.

It was flowery, poetical, and, he hoped, exactly
the type of appreciation which a Courtesan of any
nationality would like to receive from a man on whom
she had bestowed her favours.

Jacques's eyes twinkled when he finished reading
it.

"Excellent!" he said. "It is hard to believe that
you have any English blood in you."

"You are insinuating that the English are unde-monstrative," André said. "If you ever come to England, you might be surprised!"

As he spoke, he was thinking of the women who had responded to his love-making if not with the same physical ardour as Orchis, then certainly with some of the passion which he had imparted in his letter.

"I will have a servant take your letter, along with the bouquet I have chosen of the most exotic orchids, to the Habitation Leclerc as soon as you have left the city," Jacques said.

"You are thinking that Orchis might wish to see me again in person?" André questioned.

"She seldom allots a man more than one night," Jacques replied, "but she is unpredictable, and one never knows."

"You are wise to take no chances," Kirk said.

"I am trying to anticipate every eventuality," Jacques said, smiling. "Having known Orchis for many years, I know that where she is concerned it is wise always to be prepared and on one's guard."

As the servants carried André's pack from his room down to where his horse was waiting, he said:

"Please let me pay you what I owe for the horse, the flowers, and any other expenses you have incurred on my behalf."

Jacques smiled.

"It is all part of what is due to my friend Kirk," he replied, "and as I owe him my life, how can I possibly assess anything so valuable in terms of money?"

They all laughed.

But when André would have insisted on paying, Jacques brushed his words aside, and he felt that if he insisted further, he would offend the Mulatto.

André could understand, because, as Jacques had said, Mulattos lacked confidence owing to the way they were bred and the way they were treated. It gave them pleasure to think that they were important to a white man.

In fact, in this instance André would have been completely lost without him.

It was therefore an unaccustomed feeling of superiority which made Jacques determined that André should be successful in his quest and that the disguise he had given him should not be penetrated.

He waited now until the servant was out of the room, then he said:

"In your baggage I have put a bag containing powder from the bark with which I stained your skin."

"How soon shall I need to use it again?" André asked.

"Not for a fortnight or three weeks," Jacques answered, "because I have applied it thickly. You are darker than I, and darker than many other Mulattos; but there is one thing you will have to renew every few days—the half-moons on your finer-nails."

André looked down at his hands as Jacques spoke.

He remembered that Jacques had been most particular about darkening the bases of his nails.

"You will meet many very light Mulattos," Jacques explained, "and an Octoroon can be completely indistinguishable from a white man or white woman except in one particular thing: the half-moons of their nails have a dark tinge to them."

"That is how you can tell," Kirk interposed, "whether or not they have a 'touch of the tar-brush.'"

It was an expression that was used quite frequently in England, and as André nodded to show that he understood, Jacques went on:

"Of course your nails will grow, and remember that a trace of white at the base near the cuticle where it should be brown will betray you instantly."

"I will remember," André said. "And thank you again."

He clasped Kirk by the hand and asked:

"If I reach America, may I come immediately to Boston?"

"You know you are always welcome," Kirk replied, "and my family will look forward to meeting you again. You completely charmed them!"

André turned to Jacques.

"Kirk told me it was you who informed him of

the death of my uncle and his three sons when they
were massacred. Have you any idea where they
might be buried?"

"I was informed that the whole household was
killed," Jacques replied, "your uncle, your aunt, their
three sons, a little girl they had adopted who had
taken the De Villaret name, and some friends who
had taken refuge in the house. That was all I learnt
when Kirk asked me to make enquiries."

He paused, then said quietly:

"It is not Dessalines's policy to bury those he de-
stroys. Usually they are left to rot on the ground they
once owned, or their bodies are thrown into bogs and
marshes, if there are any handy."

Jacques hesitated before he went on:

"I believe the men were tortured, but that is such
a familiar method of murder in Haiti that detailed
information as to what happened did not reach me."

André's lips tightened. Then once again he said
good-bye to Kirk, and Jacques followed him down the
stairs.

At the back of the house, in the yard, where they
would not be overlooked and their departure would
not be noticed by passers-by, there were two horses.

Holding them was a huge Negro whom Jacques
introduced as Tomás.

His black face was obviously Negroid, and yet in
a way he was savagely handsome.

His hair clustered tight to his head like thick
curly black moss and he had a low forehead over
eyes that were dark and appeared intelligent.

When he smiled his whole face seemed to light
up, and at first sight André liked him and knew there
was an honesty about him that was unmistakable.

He held out his hand.

"I am glad to meet you, Tomás," he said, "and delighted that you will accompany me on my journey."

Just for a moment the Negro hesitated. André
knew it was because no white man would ever shake
hands with a Negro, and Tomás had obviously been
told the truth about him.

Then his huge hand, so large that it completely

engulfed André's, came out, and he felt the strength
of his fingers.

"Tomás will guard you with his life," Jacques said.
"Trust him, and keep nothing secret from him."

André saw that on the back of the saddle of one
of the horses there was a large bundle, which he knew
contained his clothes.

He shook Jacques's hand again, tried to express
his gratitude, and then he and Tomás mounted and
rode out of the yard.

Almost immediately, with Tomás leading the way,
they started to climb the hill behind Port-au-Prince.

André realised that they were avoiding the busy
streets and more crowded thoroughfares and keeping
to dusty lanes which soon petered away into mere
cart-tracks.

Looking at a map at Jacques's house, André had
realised that to reach his uncle's plantation they would
first have to travel along the side of the St. Marc
Channel, then climb over the Black Mountains, to
reach the valley where Philippe de Villaret had settled when he reached Haiti.

It was clear when he looked at the map that
Jacques had been right in saying that the distance
between his uncle's plantation and Port-au-Prince was
almost the same as the distance from the plantation to
Le Cap.

It was some comfort to know, although he pre-
ferred not to meet him, that Le Cap was under the
command of Henri Christophe. In fact, it was where
he had built a magnificent house which he had burnt
down at the first sight of the French ships.

Christophe had also killed many white men, but
everything he had heard about him told André that
he was less cruel and less of a tyrant than was the
new Emperor.

In fact, Christophe, while determined to be free
of French domination, had always averred that it
would be wise to be friends with the white nations
like the United States and England, because the
Americans and the British could help them.

But for the moment Christophe, like Dessalines,

would be busily employed in fighting the Spaniards;
and André, as he set off, prayed that his search would
not take him too long.

When they were well away from the town and
moving along the coast-road at a fairly good pace,
André began to talk to Tomás.

"*Monsieur* Jacques has told you, Tomás, what I
am seeking?"

"Yes, *M'sieur,* but it not easy."

"Did he also tell you that I have what I think is a
clue to where the money may have been hidden?"

"He told me, *M'sieur.*"

André drew from his pocket his uncle's letter and
read aloud to Tomás the important sentence.

"I am sure that it means that the money will be
hidden near or in the shade of a Church," he said.

Tomás did not reply, and they rode on for a
little way before the Negro said:

"We find Church."

"There must be one," André said.

They spent the first night in a small thatched
Caille in what André supposed was a village.

It consisted of a number of wooden and mud
huts with thatched roofs, each one in its own small
plot of land, bordered by cactus-plants.

"People good," Tomás observed. "Ask no questions."

He drew his horse to a standstill, dismounted, and
went to the nearest *Caille* to talk for what seemed a
long time with an old man sitting outside it and smok-
ing a clay pipe.

When he came back to André, he was smiling.

"Good shelter," he said. "*Caille* new, but empty."

It stood a little apart from the other huts, and, as
Tomás had said, it had obviously just been completed,
for the thatch was fresh and the mud walls were still
damp.

It was clean inside, and when Tomás had laid
down a rug on which André could sleep, he thought
that they might have had to camp in a far worse place.

They had brought enough food with them to last
for two days.

"After that," Jacques had said, "rely on Tomás.

What he finds may not be very palatable, but it will keep you alive."

There was chicken, small hard-boiled eggs, and cold fish cooked in a Creole sauce which was delicious.

André ate everything that Tomás offered him, knowing that the food would not keep well in such a hot climate and it might be the last decent meal he would have for a long time.

Then, because after what had happened the previous night he was still extremely tired, he lay down on the rug, and almost before he realised that he had been asleep, Tomás awoke him, saying that they must be on their way.

There was a cup of coffee for breakfast and a dried-up French roll, but André picked an orange from a tree as he passed beneath it, and he found it sweet and juicy.

There were also as many bananas as he could wish for, and he thought that however difficult it might be to obtain the sort of food he was used to, he certainly would not go hungry.

They rode on, and now they turned towards the mountains and soon from amongst the trees they could see panoramic vistas of the country and in the distance the blue sea.

They had to ride very slowly, and sometimes the branches of the mahogany, ceiba, and ironwood trees blotted out the sunshine and the forest had a mysticism which seemed to stir the senses in a strange way.

Parakeets with brilliant streaks of crimson, jade, and yellow flashed ahead of them, and occasionally there were yellow, green, and white orchids.

They cascaded down from the branches of the trees and could be seen through the thick lianas which hung like living ropes from the sky to the ground on which they rode.

The orchids made André think of Orchis and for a moment he felt as if she reached out to him, and he could not avoid being stirred by the memory of her sensuous body, her enveloping arms, and her demanding lips.

Then mentally he shook himself free of her.

She was like the lianas, he thought, twining herself round a man, eventually constricting him so that he was no longer himself but only a slave to her demands.

That night they were not so fortunate.

The thatched-roofed *Cailles* they passed were not to Tomás's taste, and André had the feeling that he did not like the forest and was afraid of it.

At one point on the trail, and sometimes it was a very faint one, they crossed another path and there a tall pole had been erected.

From the top of it dangled a black goat, held by a rope round its horns.

Tomás had already told André that crossed tracks, or a "carrefour" as it was called, were considered sacred, and he had pointed out at one place early on their ride a small altar which had obviously been erected to some local *Loa*.

"Are you telling me that that is part of Voodoo, Tomás?" André asked.

"Yes, *M'sieur*."

The way he spoke and the expression when he looked at the *Loa* told André that Tomás was a Voodoo addict, and he said no more.

Now Tomás's expression as he looked at the black goat was one almost of horror.

"What does that mean, Tomás?" André asked, pointing.

"Voodoo, *M'sieur*," Tomás replied. "Pedro worship."

"And who is he?" André enquired.

"Pedro bad! Cuba god, black magic!"

The way Tomás said it made André want to laugh, but he knew that the Negro was entirely serious and after a moment he asked:

"Who are the good gods? The gods whom you worship?"

For a moment he thought Tomás was not going to reply, then he said:

"Damballah, *M'sieur*. Damballah *Weydo* great god. He help you."

"I certainly hope he will!" André said.

"*M'sieur* not hate Voodoo?" Tomás asked tentatively.

"Why should I?" André replied. "I know very little about it, but I believe that every man has a right to believe in the religion of his own choosing."

He saw on Tomás's face an expression which he thought was one of relief, and he added:

"I was born and baptised a Catholic, but I have friends who are Protestants, and some who are Buddhists and Muslims. They are, I believe, as good, or as bad, as I am, and accountable for their actions only to their own gods."

Tomás looked up at the goat. Then as they rode on he drew his horse nearer to André's.

"Damballah help you, *M'sieur*. Help you find where treasure hidden."

"If he can tell me that," André replied, "I would listen to him with the greatest respect and be only too willing to make any offering that might be required to express my gratitude."

Tomás nodded his head.

"Leave to me, *M'sieur*," he said, and they rode on without discussing it further.

They spent a rather uncomfortable night in a clearing in the forest, with no shelter other than the trees which towered so high above them that with their branches almost meeting over their heads, it was like, André thought, being in a great Cathedral.

He knew, however, that Tomás was unsettled and on edge, and although André slept a little, Tomás had him back on his horse at the first light of dawn.

Now there was no coffee but only a few dried-up pieces of bread and fruit for their breakfast.

As they descended sharply on the other side of the mountain, they came to a village where Tomás found someone to boil him some water for their coffee, which they carried in their saddle-bags.

The next night they were in a village where the people eyed André suspiciously and were obviously not reassured by what Tomás told them about him.

"Sometimes, *M'sieur*," Tomás explained, "Mulat-

tos make trouble. They clever. Give orders an' expect
black man obey. If refuse, Mulattos cruel."

It certainly was a country torn asunder, André
thought, and he felt sorry for the people who did not
know whom to trust or in whom they could believe.

Then at last, when he least expected it, because
it seemed to him that he had been riding for years,
they saw a valley ahead.

Tomás told André as they came down from the
mountain that this was the place they were seeking.

If the forest itself had seemed beautiful, the valley was breathtaking!

First there were the rippling cane-fields, now
overgrown or farmed in small patches obviously by
local peasants.

André could imagine what they had looked like in
prosperous years when his uncle had written to France
so enthusiastically of the great fortune he was making.

They passed derelict and crumbling sugar-mills
where oxen had once padded in circles to turn the
giant grinding-wheels.

There was field upon field in what was obviously
a very fertile valley, watered by a twisting stream and
protected by the great mountains that enclosed it.

Every yard they travelled was so beautiful that
André thought he must have passed into some strange
Paradise.

They made no attempt to stop but rode on because he knew without asking the question that
Tomás was taking him to his uncle's house.

They passed through crumbling gate-posts, and
there was a drive where the flamboyants were just
beginning to come into bloom and every tree was
covered with brilliant fiery flowers that were lovely
beyond words.

Bougainvillea wreathed walls that had tumbled
down, and climbed round broken pillars in cascades of
purple, magenta, and carmine.

There was jasmine, golden in the sun, climbing
over the trees, combined with the white calla-lilies
and bushes of orange-blossom to fill the air with an
overpowering sweetness.

They had to fight their way through overgrown shrubs until, as they turned the corner of what had once been the driveway, the house stood in front of them.

André's uncle had described with such pride the white stucco-faced mansion that he had built. It had been solidly constructed and was architecturally extremely attractive.

It had two storeys and a horse-shoe staircase at the front leading up to a wide balcony which encircled the entire first floor. But now the balcony was broken and there were gaping holes in half-a-dozen places.

Over the years the roof had lost its tiles with every gale that blew, and they were scattered in front of the house, where again there were large gaping holes which might have been due to the elements or to the work of vandals.

The front door was off its hinges, and everything was encrusted with lichen or festooned with green vines that had wrapped themselves round the pillars and over what remained of the balcony and even obscured the windows.

It was dilapidated to the point where there was a desolate depression about the whole place.

The two men dismounted and André walked into the house, moving carefully on what remained of the floor-boards.

He was not surprised to find that everything removable had been looted and each room was empty except for scattered plaster from the ceiling and broken wood from smashed shutters.

One part of the house had at some time been set on fire and there the walls were blackened. With the floors thick with dust and cobwebs hanging everywhere, there was a sad air of devastation.

André was glad to move from it back into the colourful garden with its overgrown climbers.

"There is obviously nothing left for us here," he said to Tomás.

They were the first words he had spoken since they had arrived at the house.

Then, still without communicating with each other, they returned to the garden.

"No-one come here," Tomás said. "Bad magic!"

"Magic? What has that to do with it?" André asked.

In answer Tomás turned round and pointed.

André followed the direction of his finger.

"What is it? What are you showing me?"

Then he saw that over the pillar at the foot of the steps there was something which appeared to him to be a bent branch or possibly a piece of rope.

"What is it?" he asked.

"Pedro *ouanga*—black magic—evil!" Tomás replied.

"Nonsense!" André said. "I do not believe in such things. They may be real to you, but not to me."

He spoke sharply. Then as he thought that Tomás looked upset he said quickly:

"I am sorry, Tomás. I did not mean to sound so disagreeable, but perhaps I am frightened as you are frightened by such things. Magic, black or white, is easy to believe in when you are in this country."

"Come, look, *M'sieur*," Tomás said.

They reached the pillar and André saw that what he had seen was in fact a rope.

Dyed green, about two feet long and nearly as thick as a man's wrist, the ends were bound together with coloured wool, and fastened in the bindings were feathers, chicken's feathers, red ones at one end, white at the other.

Part of the rope was covered with a white residue which flaked off as André touched it. Another part was covered with something congealed, dried, and blackened. He was certain that it was blood.

"What is it?" he asked again.

"I tell you, *M'sieur*, the Pedro *ouanga* green snake. Strong magic—Magic *Noire!*"

"Why should it be here?"

"I not know, *M'sieur*. Only 'tis known you coming."

"Me? Coming here? How could anybody know?" André asked.

Tomás's eyes turned towards the mountains, then he said:

"Everything known. Drums talk."

"Are you saying," André asked slowly and patiently, "that my arrival here at this deserted and desolate plantation might already be known by those who practise Voodoo?"

Tomás nodded.

"You are making it very hard for me to believe everything you tell me," André said.

He looked at the piece of rope and realised that it had not in fact been there for very long.

He touched the dried, dark part of it that he had thought was blood, and found as he pressed it with his fingers that it was soft and wet. It was blood!

He saw too that while the pillar where the *ouanga* lay was clear of shrubs, the one on the other side was completely covered.

There was no doubt that the rope representing a snake had been placed there recently, perhaps only this morning or last night.

"I do not understand, Tomás," he said, "but I know that I do not like it."

"No worry, *M'sieur*," Tomás said. "Find good *Papaloi*, make things all right."

"What is that?" André asked.

"Man, *M'sieur*."

"What sort of man?"

"What you call Priest—Priest of Voodoo."

André put his hand up to his head.

"Am I to understand that to take away this spell, or whatever you think this imitation snake will do to me, we have to find a Voodoo Priest who goes in for white magic?"

"That right, *M'sieur*."

"It seems to me the most utter . . ."

André bit back the words.

He suddenly remembered Jacques saying to him that if he was to play the part of a Mulatto, he also had to think like a Mulatto.

Mulattos believed in Voodoo, as the Negroes did. Very well—in for a penny, in for a pound! How-

ever strange and peculiar things might seem, he
would behave as if he were a Haitian, and if that
meant playing off one magic against the other, he
might as well agree to it.

"Where will you find this Priest—this *Papaloi?*"
he asked Tomás.

"I find, *M'sieur.*"

"Very well, I agree," André answered. "In the
meantime, let us get rid of this rubbish!"

He pulled the piece of rope off the pillar and
threw it with all his might into the thick, overgrown
bushes encroaching upon the house.

"At least it has not exploded!" he said with a
smile, but Tomás did not smile.

"Curse still there till *Papaloi* remove."

Good-humouredly André slapped him on the
shoulder.

"Then find your *Papaloi,*" he said, "and also
choose a place in the house where I can sleep tonight
where the roof is not likely to fall in on my head or
the floor to crumble beneath me."

He looked up at the house, then added ruefully:

"At least when I am asleep I can pretend that I
am master of the De Villaret plantation, sleeping in
the house to which I am legally entitled, although no-
one is likely to believe it, except you."

Tomás did not speak for a moment. Then he said
so quietly that André could hardly hear him:

"Damballah tell *M'sieur* where treasure hidden."

Chapter Three

André came from the house and walked carefully down the steps into the garden.

He had eaten a surprisingly good dinner, supplied by Tomás.

They had bought two chickens in a village they had passed through earlier in the day, and as they hung from Tomás's saddle André had wondered what sort of cook he was.

However, he thought now, he might have guessed that Jacques with his meticulous efficiency would provide him with a servant who could not only direct him to where he wished to go but who was also proficient in many other ways.

As soon as Tomás realised that André intended to stay in the house, he had begun, with make-shift brooms of shrubs and twigs, to sweep some of the dust from the floor and to pull down the cobwebs which covered the walls and ceilings.

He had worked hard to clean one room, which André fancied had been a small Salon, and then he had repaired to the kitchen.

It had not been long before an appetising aroma came to where André, having seated himself on the balcony, was peeling an orange which he had plucked from one of the trees in the garden.

He was leaving a thorough inspection of the place for the morrow, when he would feel less tired.

Today had been hard riding and he had had very

little sleep the night before, because Tomás had been
anxious to get away from the forest.

He sat there imagining what the house must have
been like in his uncle's day, with beautifully decorated
rooms, and his aunt, whom he remembered as a very
attractive woman, supervising the household with the
expertise which appeared to be the birth-right of
every Frenchwoman.

There would have been many servants, and because his uncle had been a rich man, André was certain that there was in the Habitation de Villaret every
comfort that was possible in a strange land.

He wondered if he would have liked to live in
Haiti, but if he was honest he knew that some part of
him, on which had been superimposed a veneer of
English habits and the English way of life, craved for
France.

André had been obliged to flee with his family
to England to escape the excesses of the French Revolution, but as a child he had realised the grandeur in
which his grandfather lived and the power he exerted,
as a *Grand Seigneur,* over the huge estates that he
owned and the hundreds of people whom he employed.

It seemed rather hard that his grandfather had
enjoyed all the grandeur and the glory that went with
being the *Comte* de Villaret and his Uncle Philippe
had enjoyed the power of wealth.

André now held the title but nothing else, and he
thought that if his search for the treasure failed, then
he must go back to England and try to find some sort
of employment, to keep himself and his ageing mother
alive.

He was well aware that his mother longed above
all things for him to marry.

While in normal circumstances any noble family
in France would be pleased for their daughter to be
united in marriage with the *Comte* de Villaret, he
knew that he could not contemplate an arranged marriage when he had nothing to offer but an empty title.

Every masculine instinct in him shrank from the

idea of marrying someone to whom he must feel sub-
servient because she held the purse-strings.

A dowry where a wife was concerned was one
thing; a woman who would in fact be paying for
everything, and to whom her husband must apply
even for pocket-money, was something very different.

'I will never marry,' André thought to himself,
'until I can meet my wife on equal terms.'

He was still deep in thought on the balcony
when Tomás informed him that dinner was ready.

He went through the window behind him, step-
ping over fragments of broken shutters and dislodged
stone-work, to find that Tomás had laid out his meal
on a wooden packing-case.

A block of wood was his seat and his plates were
huge leaves from the shrubs growing through the windows into the house.

However, Tomás had brought with him from his
home a knife and fork with which André could cut
his chicken. He found that this, cooked Creole-fashion,
was delicious.

Tomás had also found in the overgrown jungle
which surrounded the house a cob of sweet corn and
some small, sweet tomatoes.

André was hungry and did full justice to the meal.

There was cold water to drink, which Tomás told
him came from a well which was in a courtyard in the
centre of the house.

For a moment he was apprehensive, knowing that
in times of war or revolution wells were often pois-
oned, or, worse still, made a receptacle for dead
bodies.

But the water was like liquid crystal and André
thought that at that moment he appreciated it more
than the finest French wine.

"Tomorrow buy food, plates, cups, glasses,"
Tomás murmured, "an' brooms an' towels."

André laughed.

"I had better make you a list," he said.

Then he remembered that it was unlikely that
Tomás would be able to read.

"Tomás know what required!" the Negro said with
dignity; and André, with a smile and a shrug of his
shoulders, was quite content to leave it to him.

He took a banana which lay on a leafy plate and
peeled it, walking out into the garden as he did so.

The sun had sunk, and dusk made everything
seem strange and mysterious. There were bats flying
overhead and the first stars were twinkling in the sky.

The hot, moist air was almost like the warm flesh
of a woman. André thought of Orchis, then deliberately excluded her from his mind.

As he did so, he thought that far, far away in the
distance he heard the sound of drums.

When he listened he was not certain that he had
not imagined them.

There was only the high squeak of the bats and
the sudden raucous squawk of a parakeet in the
bougainvillea.

It all seemed part of the mystery and secrecy of
Haiti, and he tried to remember all he knew about
Voodoo, what he had read about it and the little that
Kirk had told him while they were sailing from Ameri-
ca with the cargo of uniforms for Dessalines's Army.

He remembered that during the past century a
million Negroes had been brought across the ocean
from Africa and sold in the markets of Santo Domingo.

For them a new life began with the crack of the
slave-drivers' whips and a cruelty which seemed to
André, as it did to the majority of the English people,
unbelievable.

William Wilberforce, who was trying to get sla-
very abolished, had told to incredulous Members of
Parliament stories of masters who would with impuni-
ty shoot one of their slaves simply to demonstrate the
accuracy of a pistol newly arrived from Europe, while
others would bury slaves they disliked up to their
necks and use their heads as a jack in the game of
bowls.

Kirk had told André that in the Gallifet plantation
the manager rubbed brine and pepper into the open
wounds of slaves who had been flogged.

A planter at La Grande-Rivière nailed a Negro to

the wall by his ears, then sliced them off with a razor, had them grilled, and forced the man to eat them.

One man in the Plaine des Gonaïves was nicknamed "Mr. Woodenleg" because whenever he recaptured a run-away slave he would order one leg to be cut off, and if the man survived, which was unlikely, it was replaced by a wooden one.

The most common instrument of torture was the long bullock-hide whip, and the grim word that haunted the history of the island—*taille*—meant to "cut, hew, or whittle" a man until he was a bloody mess.

Black women were whipped as regularly as black men were, and although there were masters who treated their slaves well, the slaves still had less importance than pet dogs.

Their only comfort, the only ray of hope in their miserable lives, was their rites of Voodoo which they had brought with them from Africa.

It was a magic religion, the worship of many spirits, and André had heard that Priest-Kings and Priestess-Queens, the *Papaloi* and the *Mamaloi*, had the power of bringing the dead back to life in the form of *zombies*.

This he had never believed, but now he found himself thinking that in this hot, stifling climate it was easy to believe many things which he would have laughed at when he was in England.

The Revolution had been started through Voodoo, which became the heart of a secret society that linked all slaves on all plantations.

The *Papaloi* and *Mamaloi* were natural Leaders recruited from amongst the superior house-slaves or *commandeurs*.

They were the drivers who whipped the others to work in the fields.

It was one of these *commandeurs*, a British-born slave named Buckman, who led the first uprising in the great Plaine du Nord.

Buckman used the Voodoo network to synchronise the risings throughout the island.

During June and July of 1791 there were out-

breaks of disturbance in the Western Provinces. Men
were whipped, broken on the wheel, and hanged.

The planters did not regard these isolated inci-
dents as being anything important. Then at the end of
July Buckman summoned his conspirators from each
of the northern plantations, to impress upon them the
need for unity.

They met in a great wood amidst the thunder-
claps of a storm which they believed heralded the
approval of the gods, and Buckman performed the
Voodoo rites.

His *Mamaloi* slit the throat of a black boar, and
with their lips red with its blood the conspirators
swore an oath of allegiance to Buckman and his lieu-
tenants, and he set the date of the uprising as August
22.

On that night Buckman the slave-driver summoned his followers on the Turpin plantation not with
a whip but with a torch, and across the whole of the
northern plain the slaves began to burn, rape, and kill.

By the glow of the fires in the mansions and the
burning of sugar-cane they hunted out their cruel
masters to torture and kill them with a violence that
was understandable.

On some plantations, the slaves remembered past
kindnesses and smuggled their masters and their masters' children to safety.

On others, no whites escaped and no-one was left
to tell what had happened.

Odeluc, the manager of the Gallifet plantation,
who had behaved with a unique cruelty to his flogged
slaves, had heard at Le Cap that something was occurring and set off for his plantation.

He took a few of the town guards with him to
stamp out any disturbance, but when he arrived at his
plantation he found that his own slaves were amongst
the Leaders of the uprising, and they carried as a
banner the naked body of a white child impaled on a
stake.

Odeluc was captured and killed, and by now it
was unnecessary to sound an alarm, for exulting bands

of slaves, intoxicated with revenge, spread like a forest
fire across the plain.

André felt as if he could see it all happening.

What was surprising was that, having gained
power, having actually declared independence and
proclaimed himself Emperor, Dessalines, along with
Christophe, had outlawed the Voodoo which had been
instrumental in bringing him to power.

It was something André could not understand, but
he was sure it was unlikely that Voodoo, despite the
fact that it had once again gone underground, could
ever be torn out from the hearts and imaginations of
those who believed in it.

Dusk deepened into night and Tomás came onto
the balcony to say:

"Bed ready, *M'sieur*."

With a smile on his lips, André went into the small
Salon, expecting to find his blanket laid on the bare
floor as it had been the previous nights.

He was only hoping that the profusion of green
lizards which ran up the walls would not keep him
awake.

Then by the light of a flickering candle which
they had brought with them, set on the wooden
packing-case which he had used as a table, André
saw that from somewhere in the empty, desolate house
Tomás had found a native bed.

It consisted only of four pieces of wood on legs,
with the empty spaces filled in with roughly executed
webbing like a hammock.

It was the type of primitive bed that was used by
servants and slaves in every hot country, but André
knew that tonight at any rate it would be extremely
welcome.

He had thought while sitting on the balcony that
he had heard the sound of hammering.

He now saw that Tomás had obviously mended
the bed, which must have been broken for otherwise it
would certainly have been stolen, not only with some
rusty nails but with twine which held the framework
to the legs.

"*M'sieur*—careful!" Tomás warned. "Tomorrow make strong."

"Thank you, Tomás," André said. "It was very ingenious of you to have found anything, and it will certainly prove more comfortable than the ground last night."

Tomás smiled broadly at the praise, then he pulled off André's riding-boots and picked them up with his other clothes, preparatory to taking them from the room.

"You will need the candle," André said.

"Enough light in kitchen," Tomás replied. "*Bonne nuit, M'sieur!*"

André lay down rather gingerly on the bed and pulled the light rug over his nakedness.

He thought to himself that it was strange for him to be lying here in his uncle's home, waited on by a Negro servant, and wondering what adventures lay ahead of him tomorrow.

'I have been lucky, extremely lucky so far,' he thought.

Then he remembered the Pedro *ouanga* which had encircled the broken post.

Whatever Tomás might say, he could not believe that it applied to him.

How could anyone have been aware that he intended to stay there the night, and that he had in fact journeyed to the De Villaret plantation for a special purpose?

'It is a lot of bogey-tales to frighten children!' he thought, and his eyes closed.

❋   ❋   ❋

Hours later André woke to find that his candle had guttered low, and he thought as he opened his eyes that he had been unnecessarily extravagant not to have extinguished it before he went to sleep.

Then he wondered if in fact he had been afraid of being alone in the dark, but he told himself that it had been nothing of the sort, just carelessness.

Through the window which opened onto the balcony he could see a faint light from the stars overhead and there was a fragrance in the air which he knew came from a special exotic flower whose perfume was strongest at night.

It was then that he became aware of the drums.

They were closer, far closer than they had been earlier in the evening when he had not really been sure he heard them.

Drowsily he wondered what message they were sending.

Could he really credit that they might be speaking to him?

Because he was curious, he rose from his bed and walked across the floor and onto the balcony.

He moved carefully because the balcony was, he felt, none too sound and he might find himself falling onto the ground beneath.

Now he could hear the drums very clearly. They were still some way away, up in the forest, he thought, in the direction from which they had ridden.

He wondered if he should call Tomás to draw his attention to the sound.

Then even as he thought of it, some sixth sense, some inner conviction, told him that Tomás was not in the house and that he was alone.

He had nothing to substantiate such an idea, and yet, because he felt sure at this moment that it would be useless to try to attract the attention of the servant, he turned and went back to bed.

He lay for a long time in the flickering candle-light, listening, wondering, and feeling undeniably curious.

* * *

André woke in the morning to the smell of coffee, and a few minutes later Tomás came into the room carrying the mug they had used on their journey, filled with the steaming dark liquid which André drank with delight.

Tomás also brought him his clothes, and he saw that his boots had been cleaned and polished and his other things brushed.

There was a clean shirt for him to put on, and

when he was dressed Tomás served him with a breakfast of eggs and fruit and more coffee, although he had to take the cup to the kitchen to refill it.

When André had finished eating his eggs, as he had the chicken the night before, from a leaf-plate, Tomás said:

"Go find food; *M'sieur* stay here."

"Why?" André asked automatically, already knowing the answer.

"*M'sieur* not be seen."

"I agree," André said. "And here is some money, and if you want more charge it to me."

"Charge it?"

He saw that Tomás did not understand, and he said quickly:

"No—credit is not a good idea in these parts. Take all you think you will need, but if you buy too much, the local inhabitants will suspect that you are setting up house."

Tomás grinned, but André had the idea that while Tomás did not think it wise for him to be seen in the village or wherever he was going to purchase what he required, they would already know that he was here and in the house which had been empty and desolate for so long.

There was, however, no point in asking a lot of questions until Tomás had discovered what was taking place locally.

As the Negro rode away, André, hatless and with the sleeves of his white shirt rolled up for coolness, walked into the garden.

The sun was rising and it was already growing hot, but there was plenty of shade under the trees, and André was determined to explore as much as he could while obeying Tomás in not letting himself be seen.

It was difficult to discover where the cultivated garden had been or to find, in a tangle of weeds, where the vegetables for the house must have been grown.

But André looked over the grounds and thought once again how sad it was that everything had been

left to go to seed and grow as wild and savage as only
nature can be when it is left untamed.

The sun grew hotter and André moved again into
the shade of the trees.

Now he saw the parakeets beating the air with
their wings and had glimpses of orchids, although not
in the same profusion as they had been in the depths of
the forests which he and Tomás had passed through
yesterday.

He walked on, finding the beauty of the whole
place seeping its way into his imagination, and he
found himself thinking thoughts he could not understand, and yet being intrigued by the sensations they
aroused in him.

He walked for quite some way, his footsteps
muffled by the thick moss that grew beneath the tree-
trunks and which also covered what he was certain
had once been a path leading from the house.

He was interested to see where it would end.

Then suddenly, as he avoided the branches of a
shrub covered with blossoms, he saw just a little ahead
of him a white figure.

He stopped where he was, remembering that
Tomás had said he should not be seen, and wondering
who was approaching.

Then he saw that in fact the figure was not moving.

It was a Nun, wearing a white garment that
André thought must be peculiar to Haiti, for he had
seen Nuns dressed like her moving about the busy
streets of Port-au-Prince.

Her dress was white, and instead of the traditional veil and wimple, she wore a white turban on
her head, completely covering her hair and her ears.

Greatly surprised, he saw that the Nun, seated
on a fallen tree-trunk, was not alone.

Round her, perched on her outstretched hands
and on her shoulders, were birds.

She was obviously feeding them, for those on her
hands were picking at what lay in her palms, and those
on her shoulders, fluttering down on her arms or resting for a second on her head, were trusting her.

It was a picture so beautiful, so extraordinary, that it held André spellbound, and he stood watching the Nun from a distance.

Then slowly and softly, so that there would be no possibility of his being heard, he crept a little nearer.

Hidden by the shrubs and the trunks of the trees, he was now close enough to see more clearly.

As he looked at her face, upturned towards the birds, which had now been joined by many more, he realised that she was in fact very beautiful.

What was more, she was white!

Was it possible, he asked himself, that there was a white woman here, living on the De Villaret land?

Then he told himself that perhaps as a Nun she was safe.

Even so, it seemed unlikely that the Emperor and those who followed him would consider any white woman sacrosanct, whatever her religion.

Yet there was no doubt that the Nun was white and extremely beautiful.

She must be very young, André thought; at the same time, he could not remember when he had ever seen anyone quite so lovely.

Her eyes as they watched the birds seemed to fill her whole face, and her straight little nose, the sweep of her chin, and the curve of her lips made him sure she was well-born.

There was something so delicate about her beauty that he told himself that the blood in her veins could not be anything but that of an aristocrat.

Then he almost laughed aloud.

What aristocrats had been left in Haiti after the Revolution? And for that matter, what white people had survived, except those in the North, who were now being assaulted by the Emperor or the workers and armourers such as he had heard were employed in Port-au-Prince.

He wished he were an artist so that he could set down on canvas the beauty of the scene in front of him.

The small birds, some with yellow plumage, were joined by two resplendent parakeeets.

They fluttered in the air over the Nun's head and swept down on her hands, pushing aside the birds perched there to snatch the corn, or whatever it was she offered them.

She gave a little laugh of sheer amusement.

"You are both greedy and rough!" she cried. "You must take your share on the ground."

She moved her hands to scatter the grain which she drew out of a bag at her side, and the parakeets fluttered down as if they were not in the least afraid, and soon they were joined by half-a-dozen other birds.

André realised that she had spoken pure and perfect French and there had been nothing Creole in the words she had spoken or in the softness of her voice.

She put some more grain into her palms and held them up again and the small birds who had fluttered away for a moment in dismay, attacked by the parakeets, were back again.

She had three on one hand and four on the other.

She watched them with a smile which made her seem even more beautiful than she was before.

Because he felt he must speak to her, must ask her who she was, André stepped slowly from behind the bush that had concealed him.

He had taken only two steps forward when the birds were aware of his presence and rose in a cloud to sweep away into the branches of the trees above them.

For a moment the Nun followed them with her eyes, a surprised expression on her face.

Then she turned her head in André's direction and saw him.

For a moment she was very still, as if turned to stone. Then he saw an expression of terror on her face, and with a little cry that was a sound of pure fear she jumped to her feet.

"No, *Mademoiselle*, please do not go!" André cried out, but it was too late.

The Nun, running with a speed of which he would not have expected her capable, was disappearing between the trunks of the trees.

He had several glimpses of her white dress farther

and farther in the distance, then as he reached the place where she had sat, he could see her no more.

"Damn!" he said to himself. "I did not mean to frighten her."

Even as he swore, annoyed at having missed the opportunity of speaking to the Nun, he told himself that it was not surprising that she had been afraid.

To her, he was not a white man approaching a white woman, but a Mulatto, and a rather dark one at that.

'I had forgotten,' he thought ruefully, 'and I suppose being here alone and knowing what happened to the white women of Haiti during the Revolution, she would obviously be afraid, in fact terrified!'

There had been no doubt that her fear was very genuine, and at the same time, gazing rapturously at the birds she fed, she had been breathtakingly beautiful.

"I must find her again," André said to himself; then another thought came to him.

If there was one Nun there would be others, and if there were Nuns there would be a Church or a Convent.

This was exactly what he was seeking. This was the next step towards finding the treasure which his uncle had hidden in the shadow of and under the protection of God.

It would be a mistake, he decided, to follow the Nun immediately, and he also thought it was only fair that he should tell Tomás what he intended to do.

He walked back to the house, and it was only half-an-hour later when Tomás returned.

Both he and his horse were laden with what he had acquired, the most unexpected being four live chickens and a cock.

André smiled at the sight.

"I presume you are planning that we shall need their eggs," he said.

"Not lay, we eat," Tomás said with logical simplicity.

He had managed to buy, with an amazingly small amount of money, not only food but twine, nails and a hammer, cooking utensils, plates, cups, a coffee-pot, and a large knife.

It was a sharp, dangerous weapon, which the Haitians used to cut their sugar-cane.

Tomás looked pleased with his purchases, and André, quite content to let him have what he wished, smiled.

"If we are really staying here for any length of time," he said, "I think you will want more than that."

"Start little," Tomás said, "or people ask questions."

This was irrefutable, and André, eager to ask his own question, said:

"Did you know there was a Convent near here?"

He thought Tomás did not understand, and he went on:

"Nuns. I have seen a Nun in the forest."

"Come from Church," Tomás said.

He pointed in the direction in which the Nun had run away, and added:

"Church there."

"Then I shall go and look at it," André said. "Will you fetch me my horse?"

He felt that Tomás was going to expostulate and suggest that it might be a mistake; but he had every intention of going, and, as if he knew that that was how he felt, Tomás said no more.

He merely fetched the horse from the stable, and André, who had put a cravat round his neck and pulled down his shirt sleeves, mounted it.

He wore a hat, because the sun was hot, but no coat.

Then he rode off down the overgrown drive, knowing that he was keeping to the direction in which the Nun had escaped from him.

At the end of the drive he climbed a little way up the mountain and found the path which he had discovered earlier.

He had to ride slowly and had difficulty in preventing his hat from being swept off his head by the long branches.

He also had to get past or over the trunks of trees which had been blown down by the wind or had fallen from old age.

Then, sooner than he expected, he saw what he sought, a structure that could only be a Church.

It was surrounded by trees, built on a small rise above a plantation, amidst a cluster of dilapidated mud huts that had long since lost their thatched roofs.

The Church itself, built of stone and, André guessed, very much older than his uncle's house, was so overgrown with creepers that it seemed almost as green as the trees that surrounded it.

But there was no mistaking that it had once had a pointed spire, although little of it was left, and the roof had been repaired in various places with odd pieces of wood held in place by big stones.

It gave the Church a somewhat raffish appearance. At the same time, André thought it was undoubtedly what he sought.

It suddenly struck him that because it was old, because it must have stood here for perhaps a hundred years or more, that might have been why his uncle had built his house near it.

He wished now, as he had wished many times before on his voyage to America and from America to Haiti, that he had been able to read the letters which his uncle had written so frequently to France.

They of course had been left behind when his own family had escaped to London at the time of the French Revolution.

When his father had written to inform his mother of the disaster that had overcome them, they had received only a few letters before there was an ominous silence.

Whatever the explanation of his uncle's actions when he first came to Haiti, what was important now, André thought as he rode forward, was that he had found the Church where his uncle must have buried his money.

He had, however, a feeling of dismay over the fact that whatever the Church might have been like ten years ago, like everywhere else, the vegetation had increased until it seemed, except in the front, that the building stood in the forest itself.

It would be difficult under the circumstances, to know how the shadow of the Church would have fallen on the ground, which was now thickly covered with shrubs and small trees.

André imagined that their roots would be entwined in a complex fashion which would make it hard if not impossible to dig, unless the whole luxuriant surroundings were cleared.

It certainly seemed an imponderable problem at the moment.

He reached the Church, and, seeing the door standing open, he dismounted.

He tied the bridle of his horse to a post which might have been set there for that very purpose.

He again looked round him and saw that the broken *Cailles* which he had seen in the distance were farther from the Church than he had first thought.

Perhaps originally it had stood in the centre of a native village, but if that was so, the inhabitants had all left.

Now there was only the Church.

Then as he looked in an easterly direction he saw a long, low building, which had been obscured from him before by a huge frangipani tree.

The walls were plastered with white stucco, as his uncle's house had been, but it was in good repair. The shutters which covered the windows were not broken.

There was a door in the centre of the building and a brass bell outside it which was brightly polished.

'That is where the Nuns live,' André thought to himself.

However, he thought that they could wait—even the lovely Nun who had fed the birds—because he wished to inspect the Church first.

He went in through the open door and realised that he had been right in thinking the building was very old.

The walls were of rough stone, but in the chancel there were colourful murals which both delighted and intrigued him.

When he had stayed with Jacques, he had been able to examine some pictures which were in his house and which were quite unlike anything he had ever seen except in Museums in England.

They were brilliantly coloured and roughly drawn, and yet they had the same touch as had been achieved centuries before by the Italian Primitives.

When he had shown interest in the pictures, Jacques had explained:

"Haiti has a history of pirates and cut-throats, but it also could have had an artistic sense, if it had ever been developed."

"What do you mean by that?" André had asked.

"Some of the Mulattos, like myself, have seen pictures in other parts of the world and have wanted to see what they can do themselves as artists. This is the result."

"The paintings are unusual, and obviously the Mulattos are untaught," André said, "but although I am not an expert, I should have said they had talent."

"That is what I think," Jacques replied. "One day I shall take some of these pictures to America, or Kirk can do it for me."

"I doubt if the Americans would appreciate them," Kirk replied. "Let André show them in England."

"Or better still, in France," André said with a sigh.

Now he remembered the conversation and saw that the murals on the walls were very like Jacques's pictures: primitive representations of the Saints and angels, of the Virgin Mary and the Holy Child, and of Christ crucified.

The drawings, though crude and exaggerated, were brightly coloured, and André felt that those who worshipped in the Church would be uplifted and inspired by them.

He was so intent on looking at the murals that it was with a start that he realised that a Nun had come from another part of the Church to stand beside him.

"What do you seek, *mon fils?*" she enquired.

He looked at her and saw that she was a Negress. She was also so old that her wrinkled skin was almost silver, and her dark eyes seemed lost as they receded into her skull.

She wore a white habit with a wimple and veil. A rosary with a large crucifix swung from her waist.

She had spoken quietly and there was very little expression in her voice, but as André looked at her eyes he knew that she was afraid.

"I came to pray, *ma Mère,*" he replied, and he thought that a little of her fear receded.

He looked at the murals again.

"I was also admiring your decorations," he said.

"When we repaired our Church we had no money, and recently one of the Sisters has tried to decorate the walls," the Nun explained.

"When you repaired the Church?" André repeated. "What happened to it?"

He thought the question made the old woman anxious, and for a moment he felt that she was debating whether to answer him or tell him to mind his own business. Then she said:

"Those who are inflamed with a desire for violence do not always respect the House of God."

André was sure then that the Church had been damaged at the same time that his uncle's house had been fired and looted and the De Villaret family massacred.

"Could I talk to you, *ma Mère?*" he asked.

"What about, *mon fils?*"

"About what happened here and on the De Villaret plantation," he replied. "Let me explain: my name is André de Villaret, and the *Comte* Philippe de Villaret was my natural father."

The Nun made a movement with her head as if, seeing the colour of his skin, she accepted such a possibility. Then she said:

"The *Comte* was a kind, generous Patron. He built our house for us when we came here from *Le Nord.*"

"And when was that?" André enquired.

"In 1791, when the uprising began."

He remembered how he had recalled last night that Buckman's revolution had begun in the North.

"We were safe here," the Nun said, "safe until ten years later when our Patron lost his life."

There was a touch of horror in her voice that was unmistakable, and one of her hands went out tremulously to clutch the crucifix on her rosary as if she felt that it gave her protection from her own thoughts.

"What happened to you and your Nuns?" André asked gently.

"Most of us escaped by hiding in the forest," the old Nun answered.

"Most of you?"

For a moment he thought she was not going to answer him. Then she said in a whisper he could hardly hear:

"They would not let *les blancs* go."

He knew then that the white Nuns had been killed, or worse.

In which case, who was the Nun he had seen in the wood, the Nun who had run away from him?

He debated whether he should mention her, then decided against it.

As if the memories she had evoked made her feel weak, the old Nun sat down in one of the choir-stalls and André seated himself beside her.

"It was a terrible experience!" she said. "Terrible! But *le bon Dieu* protected us, and when everything was over we came back to find that although the Church had been damaged, our house was almost as we had left it."

"That was fortunate," André said.

"We were very grateful to God," the Nun said simply.

"And now? What is happening to you now?" André enquired.

The Nun looked at the cross on the altar, and, following the direction of her eyes, André saw that it was carved rather roughly from wood.

He knew without asking the question that all the Church had possessed—the cross, the candlesticks, the communion cup, and anything else of value—had been stolen.

"I think we are safe here," the Nun said in a low voice. "Henri Christophe is a good Catholic, but the Emperor . . ."

She stopped as if she knew she was going to be indiscreet, and her withered grey lips were trembling.

"The Emperor loathes the whites and does not like the Mulattos," André said, "but some of us are useful to him and so our lives are spared."

Although he did not wish to add to her fears, he had to ask the question.

"In your community of Nuns," he said, "of which I imagine you are the Mother Superior, are they all Mulattos or Negroes?"

There was a moment's pause. Then in a voice that was flat and quite expressionless the Nun replied:

"All of them, *Monsieur!*"

Chapter Four

André rode back to the house deep in thought.

He knew that the Mother Superior had been lying; at the same time, it would have been difficult for him to confront her with the fact that he had seen in the wood a Nun who was white-skinned.

He wondered if, after fleeing from him in terror, the Nun had related what had frightened her, and if in fact the other Nuns had been expecting to see him in the vicinity.

He was almost certain, however, that the Mother Superior had at first looked at him not only with fear but with surprise. Yet that thought got him nowhere.

"Another puzzle in this bewildering, mysterious land," he told himself.

He lingered on the way back to the house, looking over the plantation, seeing where his uncle must have grown cotton, where there were several thick groves of bananas, and where the sugar-cane, now completely out of control, must have been an extremely profitable crop.

He wondered why the new Emperor or Henri Christophe had not sent their own Negroes to attend to the plantation.

Then he remembered hearing that the slaves now thought themselves free, and, having cast off the yoke of one master, they did not wish to work for another.

What every ex-slave wanted was a small *Caille*

somewhere where he could live alone with his family, with just enough land to grow vegetables to feed them.

It was getting on in the afternoon when finally André rode his horse to the back of the house where stood the stables, dilapidated and mostly roofless but still capable of forming some sort of shelter for their two horses.

He knew, seeing Tomás's horse there, that the Negro was at home, and he walked into the house to find him arranging their new plates on the packing-case which served as a table.

"You are not preparing a meal as early as this, are you?" André enquired.

"*M'sieur* eat now, then go meet Damballah."

André looked at him in surprise.

"You mean you have arranged a Voodoo ceremony for tonight?" he asked.

He did not need to wait for the answer. He knew now where Tomás had been last night and why the drums had seemed so near.

He thought at least he would learn something about Voodoo, although whether Tomás's optimistic idea that it would solve all their problems would be justified remained in the lap of the gods.

Because he was hot from riding, he went down to the well and washed himself by pulling up bucket after bucket of the crystal-clear water.

Later he inspected his body carefully to see if the dye was wearing off but he was satisfied that Jacque's bark had been very effective and it was unlikely that any stranger would suspect for a moment that he was a white man.

At the same time, he could not help realising in all seriousness that if he was discovered to be an imposter at the Voodoo ceremony, his life would be forfeit even if he was not immediately made into the sacrificial victim.

Dressed in fresh clothes, he ate an excellent meal and thought once again that he was fortunate that Tomás was such a good cook.

Then, without discussing it any further, he found that the servant had brought the two horses to the front of the house.

He walked down the steps and they rode off, taking, as André had expected, the route which led in the same direction from which they had come.

They soon found themselves in the thick of the forest, and when they had gone a mile or so the tropical night descended on them.

There was a flash of vivid colours in the sky, the shifting of orange, crimson, green, and heliotrope, then as they rode on it changed into blue which in turn became amethyst.

There was the squeak of the bats overhead and the flutter of wings as they disturbed some birds that had already gone to roost.

Then, so quietly and insidiously that he was not conscious of it, yet André was certain that it had been there for some time, there was the beat of the drums.

The sound grew louder and seemed to echo all round through the trees, from the mountains which towered above them and down into the darkness of the valley, now like a deep pool spreading out below them.

The stars came out in the sky, twinkling at them through the thickness of the branches overhead, and André rode behind Tomás.

He had no idea where he was going, while Tomás moved with a surety which he thought came from his hearing rather than from his eyes.

The night became alive to the moving, throbbing, pulsating sound which seemed to André to carry a message, but what it was he could not understand.

They were now quite high up the mountain, and unexpectedly Tomás drew his horse to a standstill and dismounted.

André hesitated a moment, then did the same, and without speaking Tomás took the bridles of their horses and led them away.

A trunk of a fallen tree had a dead branch sticking out at right angles, and to this Tomás tethered

the horses, then went back to where André was waiting for him, and walked ahead.

Through the darkness André saw flickering
lights, and the drums grew louder and louder, seeming, he thought, to beat upon his ear-drums until the
vibration of them was almost unbearable.

Suddenly there was a clearing ahead, and André
stopped because he saw that there were bodies moving against the lights, seen for a moment and then lost
in the surrounding darkness.

Tomás sensed his hesitation and looked back.

"Come!" he whispered, and because André was
ashamed of himself for being slightly afraid, he followed him.

A moment later they were on the edge of a clearing in the centre of which there was a high pole or a
tall tree, André was not sure which. Beneath it, lights
flickered from shallow bowls of oil.

So suddenly that it made him start, a fire burst
into flame at the foot of the pole, and now blending
with the sound of the drums there were human voices.

For a moment it seemed as if a great multitude
shouted with all the force of their lungs, strange,
screaming sounds that were in a way a challenge to
fear and at the same time the instigation of it.

André felt Tomás's hand pulling him down on
the ground, and as he sat beside the Negro, the dancing began.

The fire blazed higher and now André could see
an old woman, naked to the waist, beginning to
dance.

He guessed she was the *Mamaloi*, and a moment
later a man girded only in a crimson loin-cloth started
to trace on the ground an intricate pattern with
corn-flour.

From where André was sitting, he could see the
Papaloi's fingers making a strange twisting and turning pattern which had a serpent-like appearance.

Though it meant nothing to him, he knew from
what he had read that it was an invocation to the
special gods whose favour they solicited.

Now the high-pitched chanting of the dancers

grew louder, and those who were watching, like
Tomás and himself, moved their bodies instinctively,
following the rhythm of the drums.

It was a weird sensation to listen to the unin-
telligible words which came from the dancers, who
were now shaking, shivering and twisting their bodies
in an almost hysterical abandon.

Occasionally there would be a louder shrieking
howl which was, André thought, a wordless chant of
supplication.

Now as the *Papaloi* finished his pattern the
rhythm became stronger, more elemental, and André
felt as if it aroused in him strange feelings, sensual,
erotic, and at the same time violent.

The *Papaloi* strode into the firelight, wearing on
his head a turban made of multi-coloured cloths
which were coiled together into a high head-dress in
which were stuck cocks' feathers.

It was obvious that he was verging on a state of
trance, and he stood shaking his whole body and
shaking also the gourd-rattle that he held in his hand.

The dancing seeemed to intensify, and the old
Mamaloi was circled by upflung arms and stamping
feet as she held in her hands two white doves.

Their wings fluttered, and André was thankful
that the wild leaping and gesticulating of the dancers
hid what happened next.

He knew this was the sacrifice which the gods
required before they would do anything that was
asked of them, and that the doves were killed by the
Mamaloi with her teeth.

The sacrifice must have been made, for the music
was now deafening, and the *Mamaloi*, keeping what
remained of the doves in her arms, moved all round
the circle so that the watchers could see what had
taken place.

As she danced past André, he could see that the
white beads that were all she wore on the upper part
of her body were made of snakes' vertebrae.

Suddenly with a mighty roar everybody shouted
in unison:

"Damballah *Weydo!* Damballah *Weydo!*"

The roar of their voices seemed to shake the very branches of the trees above them, and as they shouted again and again, the *Papaloi* and those who attended him drank from a black bottle, then blew out white clouds from their mouths.

"That Clarin," Tomás whispered.

André knew it was a native white rum, very potent, which would burn itself not only into a man's stomach but into his mind.

The *Papaloi* moved in front of them, swaying, shaking so that it seemed as if his whole body would become mobile.

He sank to his knees, then began to writhe and groan.

A woman, one of the dancers, came to his side and threw over him what appeared to be a thick woollen blanket. She covered first his feet, then his shaking, writhing body, then his head.

Suddenly the shrieking voices stopped and the drums died down almost to a whisper.

The shrouded figure on the ground seemed to become flatter and flatter. For a moment it was still, then the blanket started to move, imperceptibly at first, then gradually the motion became more and more apparent.

The fire seeemed to die out too, and André found it difficult to see. Then a hand appeared from under the edge of the blanket, and yet he was not sure.

It seemed almost as if it were a snake's head that moved with a sensuous grace.

Then slowly out of the darkness, and yet there was just enough light to see his outline, a figure rose which should have been that of a man, the *Papaloi* himself.

But now, despite the fact that he was human, he had taken on the boneless sinuosity of a snake.

'I am being hypnotised,' André thought to himself.

Yet he could not stop looking at the figure silhouetted against the flickering light of the oil-lamps,

whose face he could not see and who had unbelievably ceased to be a man.

Then out of the darkness came a voice.

"You are here, André. That is good!"

André stiffened.

He must be dreaming. But the words were cul-
tured French and spoken in the voice of his uncle.

"You will find what you seek," the voice said,
"for Sãona will show it to you. Sãona knows where it
is hidden ... Sãono ... Sãono!"

The voice died away, vanishing into the beat of
the drums.

Now the *Papaloi* or snake was no longer standing
but was back on the ground, being covered by the
blanket, his hand disappearing last, as if it were in
fact the head of a serpent.

For a moment André felt that he could not
breathe. Then the dancing began again, the drums in-
creasing in volume, the dancers leaping across and
into the fire, which had flared into new life.

The flames leapt higher and higher against the
pole, up which a man was climbing, shrieking in
ecstasy as he did so.

André sat, stunned by what was happening, at
the same time trying to force himself to think clearly
and to believe that what he had heard was not some
wild flight of his imagination.

It had been his uncle's voice, his uncle's way of
speaking, a little crisp, besides being authoritative,
and the words had been spoken in an educated
French.

It would have been impossible for any of the
half-naked Negroes gathered here, performing the
ancient rites they had brought with them from Africa, to speak in such a way.

The *Papaloi* had risen from the ground.

He came towards André and put out his hand.

André understood and they shook hands. Then
the *Papaloi* turned to Tomás and did the same but
with a very different gesture, using what André was
to learn later was a secret sign amongst those who
practise Voodoo.

He said something that André did not hear and passed on to the man sitting next to them.

Tomás touched André on the arm.

"We go, *M'sieur*," he whispered.

André rose a little reluctantly to his feet.

He wanted to stay, he wanted to hear more, he wanted to convince himself that what had happened was true.

He saw that the dancers were becoming wilder and even more unrestrained than they had been before. A man flung a woman on the ground and his body covered her.

Then Tomás pulled André away and led him from the forest, moving back sure-footedly up the path towards their horses.

Only as they reached them did André find his voice.

"Did you hear what was said, Tomás?" he asked.

"No, *M'sieur*," Tomás replied. "Hear nothing."

"You heard nothing?" André questioned in amazement. "But you must have! The *Papaloi* when he rose from under the blanket spoke to me."

Tomás released the horses' bridles.

"Hear nothing, *M'sieur!*"

André mounted, and there was no question of talking as he followed Tomás down to the plain.

Only when they were clear of the trees and riding along the edge of the plantation did Tomás say:

"*M'sieur* blessed by Damballah. Damballah help *M'sieur*."

"If you heard nothing, how do you know that?" André asked sharply.

"*Papaloi* say you under Damballah's protection. Now all well."

"You did not realise that the *Papaloi* spoke to me of what we seek?" André asked.

"Damballah speak to heart, *M'sieur*."

That was the answer, André told himself.

He now believed Tomás when he said he had not heard anything, and his instinct told him that his uncle's voice had in fact been heard by no-one except himself.

And yet how was it possible? How could any civilised, thinking man believe that a voice could come from the dead?

He found himself fighting against an inner conviction that what he had heard was true, and what had happened was possible.

And if it was, it was too astonishing to contemplate.

Then he told himself that he had never given any thought to the girl whom Jacques had mentioned as having been adopted by his uncle and who had perished with the rest of the family.

Had her name been Sāona? If it had, he had not known of it, nor in fact did he know much about the girl.

Vaguely he remembered something that his mother had said about Uncle Philippe and his wife being very disappointed when their third child had been a son instead of a daughter.

The *Comte* had certainly not mentioned her in any of the letters which had come to England after they escaped from France, but then there had been very few letters.

He had not said much about his sons either, but only about the fears he entertained for the future of the country.

'Sāona,' André thought to himself. 'It is a strange name, and not French.'

Aloud he said to Tomás:

"Have you heard of anyone called Sāona? A woman."

"No, *M'sieur.*"

André gave a little exclamation.

"I have heard it," he said, "and I know why! It is a small island off Santo Domingo."

"Yes, *M'sieur,*" Tomás said, as if he too remembered. "That right."

"Sāona!" André repeated.

An idea came to him.

Supposing the Nun he had seen, the white girl whom he had seen feeding the birds, was Sāona?

There had been stories of slaves who saved their

masters, mistresses, or their children from the venge-
ful mobs who wished to kill them.

Could that have happened in Sāona's case?

His uncle had died ten years ago. Sāona had
been eight or nine at the time. That would make her
about the age of the girl he had seen in the forest.

That too would explain why the Mother Superior
had lied: she had been afraid that because she
thought him to be a Mulatto, he would constitute a
danger to a white Nun.

"I believe we will solve all our problems," André
said aloud with a note of elation in his voice.

Tomás smiled.

"Damballah great god, *M'sieur.*"

It was difficult, after all he had heard and seen
and with the conflicting sensations and emotions vi-
brating within him, for André to sleep.

When he listened very carefully, he could still
hear the drums far, far away in the distance, and he
felt too as if they were still throbbing inside his
mind—beating, beating.

And to their accompaniment he could hear his
uncle's voice speaking to him, telling him what he
wanted to know.

It all seemed so impossible, and yet he knew he
could not wait for daylight to prove not only if what
he had heard was correct, but if Sāona was in fact
the Nun and if she could tell him where the treasure
was hidden.

He rose early, before Tomás came to call him,
and stood on the balcony looking out into the glory
of the garden. The vivid colours of the flowers, the
shrubs, and the trees seemed to swim before him in a
kaleidoscope of beauty.

He felt in some strange way as if he had been
born anew during the night and that fresh strength,
vitality, and courage had been given to him.

The moist air was no longer enervating but acti-
vating, and he felt as if he could climb the highest
mountain and swim down into the depths of the sea
and not feel in the least exhausted.

He went to the well in the courtyard to wash,

and by the time he was dressed, Tomás was bringing
him his breakfast.

There were eggs and coffee waiting on the packing-case.

"Thank you, Tomás, for taking me to the Voodoo ceremony last night," André said. "I suppose now
the black magic of the Pedro *ouanga* cannot hurt us."

"Damballah protect *M'sieur*," Tomás said, and his
smiling face told André how happy he was.

"Now I must find out if what the Damballah told
me last night was correct," André said. "Bring me my
horse. I cannot wait any longer to find Sãona."

Tomás fetched his horse without comment, and
he watched André ride away with a smile on his lips.

Then he slowly made from some twigs of wood
and some leaves the protective sign of Damballah
and set it against the pillar on which had been draped
the Pedro *ouanga*.

*   *   *

André rode fast towards the Church and when
he reached it he wondered if he should go at once to
the Convent and demand to see the white Nun.

Then he told himself that if he did so and they
refused, she might be spirited away and it would be
impossible for him to find her again.

It would be sensible to be cautious and not forget that both the white girl herself and the old Mother Superior regarded him as an enemy because he
was a man and because his skin was brown.

He tied his horse to the post he had used before, then walked towards the Church, wondering
what he should do.

The door was open as it had been before.

As he entered he saw two women standing in the
chancel.

With a sudden excitement he realised that one
of them was wearing white, and although she had her
back to him he knew that she was the Nun he had
seen in the wood.

The other was a much older woman, a Negress,

wearing a veil and wimple, as the Mother Superior
had done.

They were staring at the murals and the Nun in
white said:

"I think the paint has begun to peel a little. I
wish we could get some better materials from Port-au-
Prince."

"Who could we send?" the other Nun asked.

"It is a long way," the Nun in white replied,
"but we know they have nothing at Le Cap that is of
any use."

"I must manage with what I have," the older Nun
said in a tone of resignation.

"Get your paints now," the white Nun said, "and
I will help you to mix them."

"I will do that," the older Nun replied.

As she spoke, she moved from the chancel and
disappeared through a door that André guessed
would lead into the Convent.

The Nun in white stood without moving, looking
up at the murals.

Very quietly André walked down the aisle, and
only when he was a few feet away from her did the
Nun hear him and turn swiftly.

Again André saw that she was more beautiful
than anyone he had ever seen before. As an expression of terror came again into her eyes, he said
hastily:

"Please, *Mademoiselle*, do not be afraid. I will
not hurt you. In fact, I need your help."

The girl facing him was tense, and he knew she
wanted to run away as she had done before. But he
stood between her and her escape, either through
the door which the other Nun had used or down the
chancel itself.

A little quiver ran through her, and he said
quickly:

"Please help me, I beg of you."

With an effort that was very obvious, she forced
herself not to move. Then she said in a voice that
trembled:

"H-how can I . . . help you?"

"My name is André de Villaret, and I have come here for a very special reason."

Her breath was coming quickly and he knew that her heart was pounding in her breast, but while she still trembled, she managed to say:

"The . . . De Villarets are all . . . dead."

"*Comte* Philippe de Villaret was my natural father."

André hated to tell this lovely girl a lie, and yet somehow he had to hold her attention and prevent her from escaping him as she wished to do.

The colour rose in her cheeks as she realised the significance of what he had said. Her eyes flickered and for a moment her eye-lashes were dark against her pale cheeks.

Because he disliked having to embarrass her, he added:

"That is immaterial, but I am convinced that you are the only person who can help me, and so I throw myself on your mercy and beg you to listen to me."

"How could . . . I help . . . you?"

"Could we sit down and talk about it?" André asked.

He thought for a moment that she intended to refuse him, then her eyes met his and he felt that somehow, against her first impulse, she now felt that she could trust him.

He moved back a little and indicated the choir-stall where he had sat with the Mother Superior.

He seated himself, putting his tall hat on the ground beside him, and after a moment's hesitation the Nun joined him.

She sat as far away from him as was possible, and she clenched her hands together as if with an effort at self-control, her knuckles showing white.

"I am staying at the Habitation de Villaret," André said in a quiet, conversational tone. "I came here from Port-au-Prince two days ago."

He paused, and although the Nun gave no indication that she was interested, he knew she was listening.

"I have heard how fine the house was and how beautiful were its surroundings," André went on. "It is very sad to find it dilapidated and looted and the plantation overgrown and neglected."

He gave a little sigh, and he had the feeling that the Nun sighed too.

"When I saw you in the forest," he went on, "I was very surprised. I did not expect to see a white woman and certainly no-one whom the birds trusted as they trust you."

He paused, then remarked:

"Perhaps you are a female St. Francis. What is your name?"

As if she found it difficult to speak, the Nun drew in her breath. Then she said in a very small voice:

"I am . . . called . . . Sister Dévotée."

"A beautiful name," André said. "And how do you make the birds so tame that they sit on your shoulders and eat out of your hand?"

It was very disappointing for him that her name was not Sãona. But he told himself that it would have been too easy to learn that she was the girl he sought.

"The birds know I . . . love them," she said after a moment's pause, "and though there is plenty of food for them, they are lazy and find it easier to take it from me than to search for it in the fields."

"I understand," André said. "And may I tell you what a beautiful picture you made with them fluttering round you. I wished then, as I wish now, that I was an artist like your friend, so that I could paint you and call it 'St. Dévotée of the Birds.'"

The Nun gave a little smile and it seemed to make her even more lovely than she was before.

"I am no . . . saint," she said, "and the Reverend Mother would be shocked that any of us should presume to be one."

"I talked with the Reverend Mother yesterday," André said, "and she told me that the Nuns have been safe here after they were driven out of the North."

There was an expression on the Nun's face that
he did not understand, and after a moment she said:

"You have not ... told me how I can ... help
you."

"Are you prepared to do so?"

"It depends. How do I know if I can be of ...
assistance unless you tell me what you ... want?"

He thought the fear was back in her voice and in
her eyes.

After a moment he said:

"May I promise you something, in all sincerity
and truthfulness, here in front of the altar? I wish to
do nothing to frighten or distress you."

The Nun did not speak for a moment, then she
said:

"I want to believe you ... but I do not think I
should be talking to you here ... alone."

"Why should it matter?" André asked. "In a few
minutes your friend will return with her paints, so
there is nothing to alarm you and nothing at all un-
conventional in our sitting here in a Church."

He nearly added: "And who could be a more
effective chaperon than God?" Then he was afraid
she might think he was being sacrilegious, and he
bit back the words.

"I have come here to the Habitation de Villaret,"
he went on, "because I believe that the *Comte,* before
he died, left something he would like me to have."

"The house is empty ... everything was taken
away after the Comte was ... killed," the Nun said.

André did not speak, and she continued:

"They smashed, burnt, or stole the pictures ...
the furniture ... everything that was there."

"How do you know?" André asked abruptly.

"That is what I was ... told," the Nun said
quickly, "and as we ran away into the woods ... we
could hear it ... happening ... it was horrible! Horrible!"

There was a sharp note in her voice that told
André how much she had been affected by what had
occurred.

He could imagine how terrifying it must have

been, whether she was with the Nuns or perhaps with the De Villaret family as they prepared to die.

"You must have been very young when this happened," he said. "How is it possible that you were here in the Convent?"

He asked the question deliberately to see her reaction.

"I had been left in the charge of the Reverend Mother," she replied. "My . . . father and mother are . . . dead."

"And you came with them from the North?"

"That was where my . . . parents lived."

André was thinking quickly.

He wanted to confront her with a straight-forward question as to whether she was or was not his uncle's adopted daughter. But he was afraid that if he did so it might close the conversation between them once and for all.

She had but to say no, whether it was true or not, and then if she left him it might be hard for him to see her again.

"It is terrible to think of what happened," he said, "so much waste, so much bloodshed, so many deaths!"

"And how will it ever end?" the Nun asked. "If the French come again there will be more fighting . . . more bloodshed."

She spoke in a soft, unhappy little voice that made André feel as if he wanted to comfort her. Almost without thinking, without considering what the answer might be, he said:

"You speak as if the French might be the enemy. What nationality are you?"

She turned her face to look at him and he thought there was something stricken in the expression in her eyes, then she said slowly and carefully:

"I am Haitian. Did you not . . . realise that I am an . . . Octoroon?"

For a moment André stared at her incredulously, then he saw the base of her finger-nails with their brown tinge.

Afterwards he could remember the sensation of

shock that had run through him at the revelation, and
at the time he had felt speechless and too surprised to
reply.

He could only stare at her nails, beautifully
shaped filbert-coloured nails, with their brown half-
moons.

He wanted to cry out that it was impossible, un-
true. Then he could remember Kirk's voice saying:

"That is how you tell if they have a 'touch of the
tar-brush.' "

The idea that the Nun was white had been so
firmly implanted in his mind from the moment he
first saw her, and all last night when he had suspected
that she might be Sāona, that he felt now as if the
very ground had slipped away from beneath his feet.

An Octoroon!

Both Kirk and Jacques had told him they were
indistinguishable from white men and women, and
now he had in front of his eyes the very evidence
that that was true.

He had also been told, both in London and in
America, although it had not been of particular interest
to him at the time, that Octoroons, like love-children
in England, were often very much more beautiful than
respectable, legitimate offspring.

The Nun was certainly a living evidence of this
theory, and the mere fact that her loveliness owed
something to her mixed blood made André feel hor-
rified.

It was not just that he was disappointed in the
fact that she was not Sāona, whom he sought.

There was something so delicate, so sensitive, so
beautiful about the Nun that he felt that she should
in fact be put behind glass and worshipped, as he
had suggested, as the Saint of the Birds.

And yet, while her father had been white, her
mother might have been a Mulatto or even an Octoroon herself.

It was impossible to speak, impossible to know
what to say, and after a moment, as if she knew she
had shocked him, the Nun said:

A Personal Invitation from Barbara Cartland

Dear Reader,

I have formed the Barbara Cartland "Health and Happiness Club" so that I can share with you my sensational discoveries on beauty, health, love and romance, which is both physical and spiritual.

I will communicate with you through a series of newsletters throughout the year which will serve as a forum for you to tell me what you personally have felt, and you will also be able to learn the thoughts and feelings of other members who join me in my "Search for Rainbows." I will be thrilled to know you wish to participate.

In addition, the Health and Happiness Club will make available to members only, the finest quality health and beauty care products personally selected by me.

Do please join my Health and Happiness Club. Together we will find the secrets which bring rapture and ecstasy to my heroines and point the way to true happiness.

Yours,

FREE Membership Offer
Health & Happiness Club

Dear Barbara,

Please enroll me as a charter member in the Barbara Cartland "Health and Happiness Club." My membership application appears on the form below (or on a plain piece of paper).

I look forward to receiving the first in a series of your newsletters and learning about your sensational discoveries on beauty, health, love and romance.

I understand that the newsletters and membership in your club are <u>free</u>.

* * *

Kindly send your membership application to:
Health and Happiness Club, Inc.
Two Penn Plaza
New York, N.Y. 10001

NAME_____

ADDRESS_____

CITY_____STATE_____ZIP_____

Allow 2 weeks for delivery of the first newsletter.

"I am . . . still waiting to hear how I can . . . help you."

Because now it did not matter, André replied:

"Perhaps I have made a mistake. Perhaps no-one here can help me. I was being optimistic, but the *Comte* once spoke in a way which made me think he had provided for my future."

"How could he do that?"

"By leaving me money or treasure of some sort or another."

"You have . . . searched the . . . house?"

"What is there to search?" André enquired. "Empty rooms with the floor-boards torn up or rotted away. I imagine that those who looted it looked in all the obvious places—under the floors, in the roof—and there is certainly no furniture to contain anything, only a packing-case on which I eat my meals."

"You are . . . certain that the *Comte* meant to . . . provide for you?"

"Quite certain," André replied, "and if I had been in any doubt, I confirmed my belief last night when I attended a Voodoo ceremony."

As he spoke, he thought that it was something he would not have said to a white woman, but the Nun was not white.

She had the same black blood in her as those who worshipped Damballah and whose hearts beat faster at the sound of the drums.

As if in fact he had shocked her, the Nun rose from the choir-stall in which they were sitting and moved to stand in front of the altar.

"Voodoo is . . . wrong for Christians," she said, "and yet here the people could not . . . exist without it."

"It is outlawed by their Leaders," André retorted.

He waited for her to speak, then as she did not do so, he went on:

"But as you are well aware, they pay no attention. You must hear the drums night after night and know what is happening in the mountains."

"Voodoo is something we should not . . . discuss,"

the Nun said. "If you cannot tell me how I can help you . . . then you will understand I have other . . . duties to perform."

He heard a coldness in her voice that had not been there before, and he felt that she was angry with him, although he could not understand why.

"Very well," he said, "I will tell you what I want. I want you to tell me if you have ever heard of somebody called Sāona."

She had her back to him, and he had the feeling that she stiffened, although he could not be sure of it.

"Sāona?"

She repeated the word and it sounded soft and attractive the way she said it.

"Yes, Sāona," André said. "She was a child adopted by the *Comte*. I was told that she was massacred with the rest of the family, but last night at the Voodoo ceremony, they spoke as if she was still alive."

"How could those who . . . practise Voodoo know anything about . . . Sāona," the Nun asked.

"I have no idea," André answered, "but the drums, I am told, carry secrets so that nothing can be hidden, at least from those who understand their message."

"They were . . . wrong," the Nun said after a moment.

André rose to his feet.

"How do you know?" he asked.

He spoke sharply, his voice seeming to ring out in the emptiness of the Church.

The Nun turned round.

"She is dead!" she said firmly. "Sāona is dead!"

*   *   *

Back at the house, André sat down on the balcony to think, while Tomás, tactfully asking no questions, hurried to fetch him a cool drink.

André thought that Tomás must have known, from the expression on his face, that his journey to the Church had been fruitless and he had not found what he wanted.

He had set off in such an elated mood, quite certain, after the revelations of last night, that he would find Sāona and his journey would end with his discovering what his uncle had buried, his inheritance.

"I was a fool to think anything could be so simple," André told himself savagely.

He had been hypnotised last night by false hopes, and he despised himself for having been hoodwinked into thinking that Voodoo was anything but a lot of "mumbo-jumbo."

He thought that when he got back to London he would make his friends laugh when he told them how gullible he had been and how, for a moment, the *Papaloi* emerging from under a blanket had assumed the appearance of a snake, the sign of Damballah.

"Voodoo, snakes, and Octoroons!" he said. "Black magic or white, the whole thing is rubbish from start to finish! How could I be such a half-wit as to be taken in by such childish nonsense?"

Tomás came with the drink and André took it from him and drank thirstily.

The Negro had mixed together several fruits, adding cold water from the well, and it was delicious.

"Give me another," André said, holding out the empty glass.

"*M'sieur* disappointed?" Tomás hazarded.

"Extremely disappointed!" André said disagreeably. "If you want the truth, I believed in your Damballah, but he has let me down."

Tomás shook his head.

"Damballah never fail! *M'sieur* mistaken!"

He walked away and André looked after him with a sullen expression on his face.

"*M'sieur* mistaken in the first place!" André said to himself, "and I have no-one else to blame for having been a credulous fool!"

He sighed.

'I suppose,' he thought, 'I should now start digging, but God knows how or where!'

He stood staring at the lizards running about his feet, until Tomás came back with another drink.

He took the glass from him and said:

"Last night, Tomás, I was hypnotised by your *Papaloi*. He told me I must find someone called Sāona. But Sāona, I learnt today, is dead. Perhaps you can tell me, under the circumstances, how I can get in touch with her."

He spoke sarcastically, but, sipping the drink, he thought how good it was and that it was not Tomás's fault that his gods had played him false.

"Damballah say you find Sāona?" Tomás asked.

He spoke slowly, as if he was trying to unravel some puzzle for himself.

"That is right," André answered. "And I will tell you something I did not tell you before. I saw a Nun in the forest yesterday and thought she was white. It seemed strange that a white woman should survive after all the killings there had been, but she looked very white to me."

He saw that Tomás was listening and went on:

"After what I heard last night, I felt certain that the white Nun was Sāona, my uncle's adopted daughter, but it turns out she is an Octoroon. Her nails are coloured, as mine are. And that reminds me, I had better tint mine tomorrow, or I may find myself in trouble."

Tomás did not speak.

He was standing still, as if he was thinking, and André told himself it was too much for the black man to comprehend.

He sighed, then in a different tone of voice he said:

"Never mind. There is still time to succeed in our quest one way or another."

Still Tomás did not speak, and after a moment André said:

"Should you not be thinking about dinner? To tell the truth, I am feeling hungry."

"Thinking about Sāona, M'sieur."

"She is dead, I tell you," André said, "and the only person who can reach her is your friend Damballah. So if you are going to a Voodoo meeting tonight, ask him where she can be found."

He could not prevent the somewhat unkind jibe and a jeering note in his voice.

Then slowly, carefully, almost as if the words were being dictated to him, Tomás said:

"Damballah find Sãona!"

Chapter Five

André walked down the steps and into the garden. There was still a mist hanging round the shrubs and the last stars were still twinkling above him in the sky.

He had been unable to sleep and finally gave up the attempt, dressed himself, and went out as the dawn broke.

All night he had gone over and over again in his mind what had happened, and he found it increasingly difficult to understand how he could have been so certain, so positive, that the Nun was Sāona, only to be cast into what he told himself was a quite unreasonable depression on finding that she had black blood in her.

After all, she was only a Nun and of no consequence in his life, unless she could help him as he had hoped she might do.

Why, he wondered, did he find himself haunted by the expression of fear in her eyes and the manner in which he knew she was trembling when he was near her?

If he was honest it always got back to the same point—that she was an Octoroon.

"It must be something to do with this damned climate, with its Voodoo and all the other bogeys that I have encountered since I came here," he told himself savagely.

He tried to empty his mind, to make himself

relax, but there in front of him was the Nun's face,
her huge eyes, the soft curve of her lips, and the
straight little nose that he had thought when he first
saw it was so aristocratic.

He tried to sweep away the thoughts of her but
found it impossible, and finally as he walked into the
garden he hoped the air would kill what he told himself was almost a touch of fever.

'I will walk,' he decided. 'Strenuous exercise is
what I need.'

But he knew that once the sun had risen it would
be too hot to move any way but slowly, as the na-
tives did.

However, he set off in a determined manner,
moving sharply with an athletic stride from the garden to the path that he had taken the first day, which
led through the forest.

He knew, although he would not admit it even to
himself, that the place where he had first seen the
Nun drew him because it was impossible to erase from
his mind the picture she had made.

He could still remember the lovely angle of her
head as she had thrown it back to look up at the
birds, and could still hear the softness of her voice
when she had spoken to them.

He walked on, trying to think of other things: of
home, of America, and of his arrival in Haiti.

He recalled going to the Habitation Leclerc with
Jacques and his first sight of Orchis.

Now, strangely enough, she no longer had the
power to move him as she had done the first two days
after he left Port-au-Prince.

Then he had had to force the image of her from
his mind, to forget the memory of her arms, her lips,
her body moving against his.

Now she seemed to have vanished into the mist
which lingered amongst the trees.

The thought of her aroused no response in him,
and with a sudden twist of his lips he wondered if
perhaps where she was concerned Damballah's protection had worked.

He had almost believed, in some secret part of himself, that the Pedro *ouanga* which he had found outside the house when he had arrived had something to do with Orchis.

If that was true, then white magic had conquered black, and the power of the *ouanga* was vanquished and Orchis with it.

He moved between the shrubs but now their exotic fragrance and the profusion of their blossoms reminded him only of the Nun.

"It should be only the lilies that make me think of her," he told himself.

Yet there was something flower-like in her beauty, something which he had thought related to all flowers.

To the brilliance of the bougainvillea, the delicacy of the jasmine, and of course the waxy orange-blossoms which had a kind of innocence about them that was so obvious in the little Saint of the Birds.

Orange-blossoms for marriage.

If he did not find the treasure he sought, then he would be unable ever to marry, and despite his mother's protests he would remain a bachelor for the rest of his life.

There would be no marriage for the little Nun either, and perhaps she had been wise to embrace chastity as part of her religion.

She was so beautiful, so delicate, and perhaps it was because she was a Nun that he had seen something very spiritual about her that he had never found before in any other woman.

Then as he was thinking of her, he pushed through thick branches which crossed the path, and there, just as if his very thoughts had conjured her up, seated where she had been before, he saw the Nun!

For a moment he thought she was a figment of his imagination, for between him and her there were wisps of mist rising from the ground, making everything seem dream-like and even more mysterious than the forest was at other times.

But the Nun was real and so were the birds fluttering round her, settling on her upturned hands and pecking at the corn she had scattered at her feet.

Without waiting to look at the picture she made, and because he had an urgent desire to talk to her, André walked on.

The birds fluttered away at his approach, but this time the Nun did not move, but sat waiting for him, her eyes very wide in her face and with an expression in them which he did not understand.

He reached her, and somehow everything he wanted to say went from his mind, so that he could only stand looking down at her as she looked up at him.

In the silence between them it seemed, although the idea was quite absurd, that they spoke without words, until with an effort André said:

"You are very early."

"I could not ... sleep."

"Neither could I."

She looked away from him, then said in a shy little voice:

"I hoped that ... perhaps you would ... come here."

"I must have known you were waiting, because I wanted to see you."

Without asking her permission, he sat down beside her on the thick trunk of a fallen tree.

There was silence, then he said:

"Will your birds come back now that I am here?"

"They might," she answered, "if you are very still."

"I would like to feed them as you do."

She gave him a little smile, then took the bag that was beside her on the tree-trunk and put it in her lap.

"Hold out your hand," she said.

André did as she told him and she poured a few kernels of corn into his palm.

"Now hold it up," she ordered.

As she spoke, she held up her other hand, also with corn in it.

For a few seconds nothing happened, then there

was a flutter of wings, and one small bird, braver than
the others, settled on the Nun's hand while several
others circled overhead.

Another bird came to her, then she put up her
free hand to place it underneath André's.

As she did so, he felt a strange sensation streak
through him, almost like a shaft of lightning.

The Nun did not move, did not take her hand
away, but somehow he knew that she had felt the
same sensation.

His heart was beating in an unusual way, and he
knew that the vibration between them was unmistakable, and at the same time inexplicable.

The birds swooped down, snatched the kernels
of corn from his palm, then flew away.

Another and yet another did the same, until one
settled on the end of his finger, to sit pecking greedily
at what he held, the Nun's hand holding his.

It was an enchantment that he had never known
before, and he knew it was not only because of the
birds but because of the girl sitting next to him and
the feelings her hand continued to arouse in him.

"I want to talk to you," he said in a low voice.

Although he spoke hardly above a whisper, the
birds heard him and fluttered away.

He dropped his hand, the Nun took her hand
away, and André threw what remained of the corn
onto the ground.

Then he turned round so that he was looking
directly at her.

"Why did you want to see me?" he asked.

The directness of the question brought the blood
into her cheeks.

She looked away from him shyly.

"Last night," she replied, "I thought I had been
... unkind and not really ... helpful. I was ashamed
... and wanted to ask your ... forgiveness."

"You felt that you would find me here?"

"If not ... I thought you would ... come back to
the Church ... sometime."

"I should have come because I should have been

unable to keep away," André said. "I wanted to see you and I thought of you all night."

His words startled her.

She looked at him swiftly, then looked away again, but he knew that there was not the fear in her eyes that had been there before.

"You are a very strange and unusual person to find here of all places," he remarked.

"Why do you . . . say that?"

"I was looking for a Church. I thought there was sure to be one in the vicinity of the house, but I did not expect to find a Convent."

She smiled.

"It is not a very large one."

"But still you are a community of Nuns."

His lips were saying one thing, but his thoughts were very different.

Now as if he could not prevent himself, he asked:

"How could you shut yourself away from the world? How could you dedicate yourself to a life where you cannot take a husband or be loved by any man?"

The Nun did not speak for a moment, then she said in a low voice:

"I . . . have God."

"Will that be enough?" André asked. "As the years go by, you will never know human love, will never hold a child of your own in your arms."

He saw a little quiver run through her. Then as if she could not bear the note of accusation in his voice, she said:

"At . . . least I am . . . safe!"

"Are you?" he enquired. "There are a great many Christians in the country, I believe, but that does not prevent them from killing one another and the Mulattos who are hated by the Emperor."

The Nun shivered and made a little gesture with her hands as if she would prevent him from saying any more.

"You are trying to . . . frighten me," she said.

"That is the last thing I want to do," André replied, "but I am upset—shocked, if you like—that anyone as beautiful as you should waste your life, when there is so much else that you might do."

The Nun sat up a little straighter.

"Prayer is never . . . wasted."

"You can pray as well as do other things," André said. "I am a Catholic. I pray when I am in difficulties; I pray when I am grateful; I pray for help; but I am also prepared to live in the world, struggle with it as it is, not to shut myself away and try to escape the reality of life."

"Sometimes it is too . . . real to . . . bear," the Nun said, as if she was speaking to herself.

"Shall I tell you something?" André asked.

She half-turned her face towards him, to show that she was listening, and he went on:

"When I first saw you, I thought, by some incredible luck as far as I was concerned, that you were the girl whom the *Comte* de Villaret had adopted and who was called Sãona."

"Why should you have thought . . . that?" the Nun enquired.

"For one thing, because you were so beautiful; another, because I believed you to be white; and thirdly, because at the Voodoo ceremony a voice told me to find Sãona, and like a fool I thought it would be easy."

"And if you had found her?" the Nun asked. "What would you have . . . done then?"

"I believe she would have shown me what I sought. Then I planned that I would take her back to England with me, to live with my mother."

"And you think she would have . . . liked that, had she been . . . alive?"

"She could hardly have wished to stay in this country, after all she had been through," André said.

"No," the Nun agreed.

She paused, then she asked:

"You live in England? I expected you to live in Haiti."

The moment she spoke André remembered that she thought him to be a Mulatto.

Because he was sitting close to her, he had been beguiled into a false security.

He had in fact completely forgotten the colour of his skin, and had spoken the truth, thinking of himself as he actually was.

Too late, he remembered that Jacques had said he must not only look like a Mulatto but think like one. But he had been thinking as André de Villaret.

Now he realised how indiscreet he had been.

"I have been living in England for a few years," he said, wondering how that would sound to the Nun, "and I have in fact come back to see if I would prefer to return here to my own country."

She did not answer for a moment. Then she asked:

"What is England like?"

"It is a very pleasant country," André replied. "Have you never met any English here in Haiti?"

She shook her head, and he thought it was unlikely that the few English there were in the country would be Catholics and therefore she would not even have seen them in Church.

"Christophe likes the English," he said, "and that is because he prefers anyone to the hated French."

"My father was French," the Nun said softly.

"And so was mine," André replied. "That is another thing we have in common."

She looked at him questioningly and he said quickly:

"Our love of birds, and our interest in paintings. Do not forget that I met you when you were looking up at your friend's murals, and of course—our blood is the same."

He felt false and somewhat of a cheat as he said the last words, but he wanted to put her at her ease; he wanted, if he was honest, for her to like him.

Suddenly the sun, which had risen, began to shine through the branches, touching everything with its golden rays.

It made everything round them seem to glimmer in an almost celestial light, and André said impulsively:

"What is the colour of your hair? I would like to see the sun on it."

As he spoke, he knew he had frightened her. She drew herself a little farther away from him, and after a moment she said:

"It must be ... getting late. ... I must go ... back to the Convent."

"I have a feeling," André said, "that you are playing truant, that in fact no-one knows that you have left."

He was sure he had hit on the truth, from the expression on her face.

"I wanted to feed the birds," she said defensively.

"And to see me?" André persisted.

She did not answer, and he had the sudden fear that she really would leave him.

"I have an idea," he said. "It must be breakfasttime. Why do you not come back to the house with me and have something to eat?"

She looked at him in astonishment.

"I could not do that."

"Why not?" he asked. "It is still very early, and I expect the Nuns will guess that you are feeding your birds and not worry unduly about your absence."

"B-but ..." she began.

"Be brave for once!" André said. "Stop running away from the world, but step right into it. Come and see the house where I am staying, and Tomás, my servant, will make us a delicious breakfast with the eggs that are laid by four very obliging little hens which we bought locally."

As if she could not help herself, the Nun laughed.

André rose to his feet.

"You will come?" he asked.

She rose too, but there was an expression of indecision in her eyes.

"I ... I ought to ... go back."

"Think how dull it will be. At least think how afterwards you will regret not being adventurous; for once, do something you ought not to do!"

He smiled and added:

"You can be very penitent later."

The Nun still did not move. She only stood looking at him, and he had a feeling that she was asking
herself once again if she could trust him.

"Please come," he pleaded, and she capitulated.

"The Reverend Mother would be . . . angry if she
knew."

"Then unless she asks you directly, do not volun-
teer the information," André said. "There is a proverb
in England which says: 'What the eye does not see,
the heart does not grieve over.'"

The Nun laughed.

"You are leading me into temptation," she said. "I
shall have to say a hundred penitential prayers for
listening to you."

"Perhaps you will feel it was worth it."

He began to move in the direction from which he
had come and she walked beside him.

After a little while the path was too narrow for
them to walk together. He moved ahead, and on an
impulse as he passed her he took her hand in his.

"It is quite rough here," he said. "You must be
careful not to fall."

It was only an excuse to touch her, and once
again as his fingers closed over hers he felt the same
lightning moving through his body, and he could have
sworn that she felt the same.

They walked in silence, until just below them
they saw the house and the breathless panoramic
beauty of shrubs and overgrown flowers surrounding
it.

The Nun drew in her breath.

"It is so beautiful!"

"I wish I could have seen it in the past," André
replied. "What was it like then?"

She did not answer, and only when they reached
the end of the path and stepped down onto the flat
part of the garden did the Nun take her hand from
his, to stand still, staring at the house.

"You remember it?" he asked, not certain why he
asked the question.

He could hardly believe that, living so near, she
had not been to the Habitation de Villaret.

"I ... I have not been here since ... " she murmured so softly that it was hard to catch the words.

"Since the *Comte* and his family were massacred?" André finished.

"Y-yes."

He saw that she was very pale, so pale that he thought she might faint, and he deliberately took her hand in his again.

"Come," he said. "If there are any ghosts, let us put them away. Let us remember that we are living today, not in the past, and not yet in the future."

He smiled at her.

"This is the adventure I promised you, and you are not to think of anything else."

With difficulty, she took her eyes from the house to look at him. Then, as if she tried to echo the lightness of his mood, she said:

"As you say ... this is today, and we are ... here."

"We are here," he repeated, "and I am hungry, as I am sure you must be too."

He drew her over the uneven ground and through the shrubs to the front steps.

As they reached them, she looked up at the broken balcony, the smashed shutters, and the creepers and bougainvillea climbing over everything.

Tomás appeared above them.

"Good-morning, Tomás!" André called. "We have a guest for breakfast!"

Tomás smiled, and there was an unmistakable expression of joy on his face as he hurried away.

André, still holding the Nun's hand, drew her up the steps and onto the balcony.

"I am afraid our furnishings are nonexistent," he said, "and so far Tomás has only cleaned one room, which has to serve as a Salon, a *salle-à-manger*, and a bed-room."

The Nun laughed and stepped through the broken window into the house.

The packing-case stood in the centre of the room, laid with the coarse white plates that Tomás had bought locally and a saucer-less cup from which André drank his coffee.

She did not say anything, she only looked round, then went to the opening where there had once been a door that led into the next room.

"Careful!" André warned. "The few floor-boards that are not missing in that room, which appears to have been the Grand Salon, are now decidedly unsafe."

The Nun stood there for a moment, then came back towards him.

"It is . . . very sad."

"Very," André agreed, "but there is nothing we can do about it, so let us talk of something else. Would you tell me how this room was furnished when you saw it last?"

She shook her head.

"I was at the . . . Convent," she said after a moment.

"Yes, of course, but you must have stayed somewhere while the *Comte* built it for you when you had escaped from the North."

She did not answer, and he thought she was being deliberately difficult, or else the memories of the massacre that had taken place four years after the Nuns arrived were still too poignant and horrible to make her feel anything but a renewal of the fear that she had felt as she hid in the forest.

However, there was no need for him to say anything, because Tomás came hurrying into the room with another large log, which he set down beside the table.

"Seat for lady," he said, smiling benignly at the Nun.

"Thank you, Tomás," she said. "That is very kind of you."

Tomás vanished again, and the Nun, seating herself at the table, said:

"He seems a nice man."

"He is a great believer in Voodoo," André said provocatively, to see what she would reply.

She gave him what was almost a mischievous little look.

"They all are," she said. "When the Priest comes

to say Mass in the Church once a month, or sometimes more often, he always preaches against Voodoo."

There was a twinkle in her eyes as she continued:

"I watch everyone in the congregation shuffling
and looking guilty, and I know if they are at Mass today they were performing Voodoo last night!"

"Tomás is quite certain that Damballah will find
Sāona for me."

"Do you believe him?"

"I did to begin with, but then yesterday when
you convinced me that you were not Sāona, I was
very disappointed and despondent."

"What will you do now?"

"I shall try to find what I believe the *Comte* left
me," André answered.

"And if it is impossible?"

"Then I shall accept the inevitable and give it all
up as a bad job."

"Then where will you go?"

He shrugged his shoulders.

"Perhaps to Port-au-Prince. Maybe to England. As
I have already told you, my mother lives there."

"And you will not come back?"

"Perhaps not. Haiti is not a very comfortable
place for a Mulatto, as you well know."

"You speak very good French," she said unexpectedly.

"Thank you. I take that as a compliment, but I
suppose we who have mixed blood have an aptitude
for picking up the best in our antecedents, even
though we sometimes inherit the worst."

The Nun did not answer, but looked round with
a smile as Tomás appeared, carrying a dish which contained eggs and a variety of different vegetables.

There was steaming coffee and also, unexpectedly, some small rolls of bread, which André thought he
must have baked as a surprise.

The Nun clapped her hands.

"It all looks delicious!" she exclaimed. "Now I admit that I feel not only hungry but greedy!"

"Then there is nothing to wait for."

André sat down beside the packing-case and as he did so the Nun said:

"We ought to say Grace."

"Then please say it," André replied.

She put her hands palm to palm as if she were a child, said Grace in Latin, then opened her eyes to say a little accusingly:

"You did not join in."

"I was watching you," he replied, "and I thought you evoked, for us both, all the blessings that are necessary on such an important occasion."

"If you are making fun of me, I shall feel guilty and return immediately to the Convent!" she threatened.

"Think what a delicious breakfast you would miss," André replied. They both laughed.

It seemed easy to laugh as they ate, and Tomás kept hurrying back to replenish the coffee and bring them more dishes he had cooked, including two ears of sweet corn.

As the Nun finished hers, she licked the tips of her fingers and said:

"I have never had such an enormous breakfast! I shall not be hungry again for at least a year!"

André gave her his handkerchief.

"Is the food in the Convent so sparse?" he asked.

"It is very plain ... and rather dull," she answered.

Then as she returned his handkerchief she added:

"That was unkind of me. Sister Marie tries so hard to cook what we like, but I am afraid she has very little imagination."

"Then while I am here," André said, "it would be a great pity not to avail yourself of mine, or rather Tomás's, hospitality. He can cook a chicken and make it more appetising than any dish I have ever eaten anywhere else in the world."

"You are lucky that you can travel."

"Very lucky. At the same time, I would like to

afford to have the sort of home of which I often
dream."

"And you need money for that?"

"That is what I hoped I might find here. Perhaps
I was mistaken."

There was silence, then the Nun said:

"Is it . . . difficult or . . . uncomfortable in . . . England to be a . . . Mulatto?"

André had an impulse to tell her the truth, that
he was a Frenchman and white.

Then he thought that because she was an Octoroon, it might make her feel uncomfortable, or, worse
still, he might put himself in quite unnecessary danger.

He could not believe for a moment that she
would betray him, but she might tell his secret to the
other Nuns, who, being Negroes, might be whole-
heartedly in sympathy with those who were now the
Leaders of the country.

Instead, after he had hesitated for a moment he
said:

"I want to talk about you. Tell me about your
family."

"I am an orphan," she answered, "and I would
rather not talk about myself. The Nuns in the Convent
dedicate themselves to Christ. He is our family and
our whole life."

André rose from the table.

"Let me show you the garden," he said. "Unless
you have any wish to inspect more rooms which are in
an even worse state and more barren and depress-
ing than this."

"I would like to see the garden," the Nun replied.

"Then I must go back."

"Be careful how you climb through the window,"
André warned.

He stepped onto the balcony and turned back to
put out his hands towards her.

She held on to him for a moment and he had an
irrepressible impulse to put his arms round her and
hold her close.

'I must be careful,' he thought to himself. 'If I am

too familiar I may frighten her, and she may run
away again.'

It was easy to understand why she had run away
from him in terror the first time she had seen him.

She had the type of beauty, he thought, that
would disturb, bemuse, and attract any man, not in
the same way that Orchis's sensuality aroused those
who looked at her, but in a much more subtle manner
that was even more inescapable.

It seemed absurd, after having known her for
such a short time, but he felt as if she belonged to
him and he could not let her go.

He wanted to hold on to her, he wanted to suggest wild, crazy things, such as to take her away from
Haiti, take her to England as he would have done had
she been Sãona.

As they walked down the steps into the garden he
told himself once again that it was the climate that
was affecting him to the point where it was difficult to
think clearly.

He was the *Comte* de Villaret, the head of an old,
illustrious, and venerated family. He had responsibili-
ties, not only towards his mother but to the De Villarets who still remained in France.

Many of them had been killed during the Revolution, but there were cousins and more distant con-
nections who bore the name and who were, he was
sure, existing somehow under the regime of Napoleon.

One day, when peace came, he would find and
help them, as was expected in his position.

That was yet another reason why he wanted money, why he wanted to be able to fulfil the obligations
entailed by blood, as his ancestors had done in the
past.

This all flashed through his mind, but he still
knew that something he could not control was forcing
him towards this exquisite girl, this Nun, and, worse
than anything else, this Octoroon.

They walked across the garden and he found that
instead of her following him, he was following her.

She swept aside some overgrown bushes and led

him until he found, to his surprise, that they were standing in what must have once been a tiny walled garden.

The walls had almost disappeared under the weight of the climbers, and the flowers that filled the beds had grown wildly in a jungle-like profusion.

In the centre there was a small circular stone pool in which stood a plump cupid holding a dolphin.

Once water must have flowed from the dolphin's mouth into the pool, and there must have been gold-fish, André thought, like those he remembered swim-ming in the fountains that played in the garden where he had lived in France.

Now there were no goldfish and no water, and lizards were running over the cracked stone.

But it was still a symbol of an elegance that must once, André thought, have been a delight for his aunt and a little girl called Sāona.

"I had not found this before," he said.

"It is . . . very pretty," the Nun said, looking at the flowers and the cupid.

"And so are you."

She looked up at him in surprise, and as their eyes met it was impossible to look away.

They just stood staring at each other. It seemed as if the whole of the small garden vibrated like the sun itself, until there was nothing else, nothing in the world but their eyes looking into each other's and somehow a part of eternity.

"What has happened to us?" André asked, and the words were almost a whisper.

The Nun did not reply, and after a moment he said:

"I want to touch you, I want to kiss you, but I know it is forbidden. I only know that from the moment I saw you, something happened which had never happened to me before."

"I . . . do not . . . understand."

Her lips moved, but what she said was somehow unimportant.

"You do understand," André contradicted. "I fell in love. I love you and I can no more control what I feel than I can fly into the air like one of your birds. And now that you are here, now that we have been together this morning, it is no use trying to pretend. You have to hear the truth."

"You . . . love me?"

"I love you!" he repeated. "I love you in a way that I cannot explain even to myself. It is just something so great, so overwhelming, that I cannot fight against it."

"I . . . I must not . . . listen to you!"

"That is what your mind tells you," André said, "but your heart says something very different. I knew when I touched your hand that what I felt, you felt too. You are mine, whatever difficulties, whatever obstacles there are between us, and all I am asking you is, what can we do about it?"

The Nun gave a little cry and then put up her hands to cover her eyes.

"I cannot . . . listen to . . . you," she said. "I must not . . . listen! Please, let me . . . go!"

"You are free to go whenever you wish," André said. "You know I would not stop you. I love you too much to do anything that would hurt or upset you."

She stood in front of him, her eyes hidden in her hands, her head bent so that he could see the soft white skin at the back of her neck.

He resisted an impulse to bend and kiss it, and as if he was suddenly pulled back into sanity, he put his own hand up to his head.

"What have I been saying to you?" he asked. "I know you believe it to be wrong. I suppose that in fact it is wrong that I should speak to you, a Nun, in such a way, but, oh, God, I cannot help myself!"

He thought she was crying, and instinctively he reached out his arms, then dropped them to his sides.

"Come," he said in a voice that was suddenly harsh. "I must take you back. What is the point of torturing ourselves?"

There was a bitterness in his voice that had not been there before.

She raised her face and he saw that there were not tears in her eyes but something else, a darkness and a distress that was somehow different from what he had expected.

"I . . . I do not . . . know what . . . to say," she murmured after a moment.

"There is no point in saying anything," he answered. "I am ashamed of myself. I should have had more self-control and should not have told you what I feel."

He walked towards the entrance to the garden, and as he reached it he realised that she was following him, but slowly, almost as if she dragged one foot after the other.

He forced his way through the shrubs, and when they reached the front of the house he waited and she came to his side.

"I apologise," he said.

"There is . . . no need."

"There is every need," he replied. "I have behaved in an abominable manner, as I am well aware. You are a Nun. You are also my guest."

"I do not want you to . . . reproach yourself," the Nun said. "It was my fault. I should not have come here, but you made it seem . . . an adventure."

"That is what it should have been."

André pressed his lips together as if to prevent himself from saying any more.

He was in fact appalled by his own behaviour.

How could he have said such things? How could he have allowed himself to upset her, when their love could have no ending, no beginning for that matter?

'I must go away,' he thought to himself.

As if she knew what he was thinking, the Nun asked:

"I shall . . . see you again?"

"I doubt it," André answered. "I feel that the sooner I return to my normal life and to sanity, the better."

The Nun gave a little cry.

"You are . . . hurt . . . you are . . . unhappy, and I did not . . . want that to happen."

"You are very generous," André replied. "Everything that has happened is my fault, and the only

blame you can take to yourself is that you are so lovely that you go to a man's head!"

He spoke half-mockingly and he knew that the
note in his voice hurt her as he had not been able
to do before.

"I am . . . sorry," she said again.

He looked into her eyes and his bitterness vanished.

Once again he felt as if she reached out towards
him, and every nerve in his body made him want to
respond.

"It is wrong from your point of view," he said
quietly. "If things were different, then there are many
things I could say; but now the kindest and the best
thing I can do is to keep silent."

"Why . . . why?" she asked.

"Why?" he echoed. "You know some of the an-
swers, and I know them too. We can mean nothing to
each other, and therefore it would only be an agony
both for you and for me to meet, to feel as we are
feeling now and know that we have to forget."

He saw in her eyes what he thought was an expression of pain, and for a moment the thought came
to him that if only she were not a Nun, he could take
her as his mistress.

They could go anywhere in the world together,
but he knew that even to suggest such a thing would
be to spoil and defame her purity, which surrounded
her like a light.

Not only because she was a Nun but because there
was something so spiritual about her, he was sure that
she was even more innocent than a girl of her own
age in London or America would be.

Clearly, knowing so little of the species, she had
not been frightened of him as a man who might try to
make love to her, but as someone who might kill her,
and that was a very different thing.

André drew in his breath.

In that second it seemed to him as if he grew
immeasurably older and wiser.

"Listen, my little Saint of the Birds," he said, "I
want you to promise me that you will forget every-

thing that has happened since you came to breakfast
with me and we laughed over the meal that Tomás
cooked for us."

Her eyes were on him as he went on:

"Forget everything but that this is a little adventure which we have both enjoyed, for which you have
played truant from the safety of what is your home
for all time."

His voice deepened as he went on:

"I want you to promise me something else as
well."

"What . . . is that?" she asked.

"That you will never, and I mean never, be alone
with any man as you have been with me."

Her eyes widened and he felt that she was questioning why he had asked such a thing, and he explained:

"You are too lovely, too beautiful, and too dis-
turbing ever to take risks with yourself. Do you understand?"

"I . . . I think . . . so," she whispered.

"I have behaved in a way that I think is repre-
hensible, but another man might have behaved in an
even more abhorrent manner and you would not have
been able to prevent him."

Now the colour swept up her cheeks and it made
her look very young and very vulnerable.

Once again André found it hard not to hold her
close, to tell her not to be afraid, to assure her that
he would protect her.

Then he asked himself from whom he should
protect her, except himself.

She looked so lovely in her white gown with the
flowers all round her, and he thought he would always
remember this moment.

Then he realised that where she was standing
there was a great clump of white calla-lilies amidst
their deep green leaves—the flowers of purity, the
flowers of the Madonna.

He knew then that he must not hurt her either by
word or by deed.

He looked at her for a long moment, then went

down on one knee, and taking her hand in his, he
kissed it.

"Forgive me," he said brokenly. "I am your very
humble servant, and one day perhaps you will understand that it has been very hard for me to do what is
right."

"You . . . must not . . . kneel," the Nun said in a
frightened little voice.

"I kneel because I love and worship you," André
replied. "Wherever I go, whatever happens in the
future, you will always be in a special shrine in my
heart, my Saint of the Birds. The Saint who asked a
blessing on me when she said Grace."

He kissed her hand again and rose to his feet.

"Come," he said gently. "I will take you back."

They walked towards the door of the house and
as they went André felt as if he had passed through
an emotional experience which left him drawn and
exhausted.

He told himself that it all seemed so unreal, and
yet he knew that he had spoken with a sincerity
which came from his very soul.

He had met the Nun only twice before in his life,
but the love he felt was so overwhelming, so com-
pelling, that he did not doubt for a moment that he
had lost his heart for all time.

They were walking across the front of the house
towards the path which led into the wood when Tomás came onto the balcony and called:

"M'sieur!"

André turned.

"What is it, Tomás?"

"M'sieur, wait!"

André, looking at the Negro, wondered what was
worrying him.

Tomás came hurrying down the steps and André
saw that he carried a small bowl in his hand and there
was a white towel over one of his arms.

"What is it, Tomás?" André asked almost irritably.

"Lady wash hands," Tomás said, holding out the
bowl to the Nun.

André remembered that after they had eaten the

sweet corn at breakfast he had lent the Nun a clean handkerchief with which to wipe her fingers.

Somewhat belatedly, he thought, Tomás had remembered that he should have provided finger-bowls for such an occasion, only unfortunately they had none.

The Nun smiled sweetly at the Negro.

"Thank you, Tomás," she said. "It was very kind of you to think of it."

She dipped her fingers into the water, then held out her hands for the towel.

Tomás handed it to her, and, having used it, she handed it back to him.

He took it from her and lifted the bowl towards André.

"I think this is really unnecessary . . ." he began, then thought perhaps it would be discouraging for Tomás if he did not do as he was asked.

He dabbled his fingers in the water, then wiped them.

"Thank you, Tomás," he said, and would have turned away.

"*M'sieur!*"

"What is it now?" André enquired.

"Look lady's fingers," Tomás replied. "Look yours, *M'sieur!*"

André looked at him in astonishment, then glanced down at his fingers.

For a moment he could not think what he was looking for. Then he saw that not only his half-moons but also the tips of his nails were white.

For a moment he could only look at them in consternation.

Then he saw that Tomás was staring at the Nun's fingers in the same way as she was.

The dark half-moons which had proclaimed her an Octoroon had vanished!

Chapter Six

For a moment André could only stare blindly at the Nun. Then she raised her eyes and looked at him.

It seemed as if she was haloed by a light that was blinding, and he said in a voice which did not sound like his own:

"You are—Sãona!"

He knew that she was finding it hard to answer him, and there was an expression on her face that he could not explain to himself.

Then she said in a hesitating voice:

"Y-yes ... I am ... Sãona ... and you ... you are not a ... Mulatto!"

"No. I am, now that my uncle is dead, the *Comte* de Villaret!"

He saw her eyes light up with a sudden radiance. Then hoarsely, as if his voice came from a very long distance, he asked:

"Are you a Nun? Have you taken your vows?"

She smiled and the sun was suddenly brilliant. Then her eyes fell before his.

"No," she said. "It was ... impossible for me to ... do so."

André reached out and took her by the arm. Tomás had vanished.

He led her with him past the calla-lilies, through the undergrowth, and back into the little garden with the stone statue.

Only as they reached it did Sãona look up at him and ask in a whisper:

"Why have you . . . brought me . . . here?"

"I think you know the answer to that," André replied.

He released her arm to stand looking down at her, at her pointed little face, her straight nose, her big eyes raised to his; and very slowly, as if he savoured the moment and at the same time was half-afraid that she was still the Saint that he dared not touch, he put his arms round her.

She did not resist him, but he felt her tremble, and he was sure it was not with fear.

"I told you I loved you," he said in a deep voice, "though there were reasons why you could not answer me then, why I had no right to declare my love. But now those reasons have gone."

His arms tightened as he said:

"I love you, Sãona! I love you, whatever you are, whoever you may be. But now I want to know what you feel for me."

Her eyes dropped and he thought it would be impossible for any woman to be more beautiful.

"I was . . . afraid," she murmured, "because you were . . . a Mulatto."

"I can understand that," André said, "but I loved you whether you were an Octoroon or had all the black blood in you that ever existed. I knew then that you were mine. But now there is nothing to prevent me from claiming you."

As he spoke, he put his hand under her chin and tipped her face up to his.

He thought as he did so that she was like a flower, a white lily so pure, so perfect, that he was afraid to touch her.

Then, because he could not help himself, his mouth was on hers.

He kissed her very gently, almost with the touch of a butterfly hovering over a blossom. Then the softness of her lips, their innocence and sweetness, made him feel as never before had he felt when kissing a woman.

This was love, he thought, the love he had never known, the love that was part of the Divine and

came to him with the same wonder and glory that he
felt belonged to God.

The pressure of his lips deepened and became
more insistent, and now he knew without her telling
him that Sāona loved him and that her lips responded
to his.

He kissed her until they became part of the sunshine and the flowers round them, the music of the
bees, the flutter of the birds, and the trees overhead.

André raised his head.

"I love you, my darling, my precious little Saint!
And I think you love me a little in return."

She gave a little murmur and turned her face
against his shoulder.

"You have told me," he said, "that you are not
really a Nun, and therefore, my precious one, I shall
do what I have always wanted to do."

As he spoke, he very gently pulled the turban-like
covering from her head.

It was a soft veil, and as he pulled it away Sāona's
hair fell down over her shoulders.

It was fair, the colour of the sunshine, and he
thought that he had always known that that was what
it would be like.

He touched her head and asked:

"Why did you not tell me who you were?"

He felt her give a deep breath, then she looked
up at him to say:

"I wanted to . . . tell you . . . my heart told me
that I could . . . trust you . . . but I was . . . afraid."

"I can understand that," he said gently.

"It was . . . the Mulattos who came after they
were all . . . d-dead to . . . search the house and to dig
in the . . . garden for what they thought must be
buried."

André understood that it would have been the
Mulattos in Dessalines's Army who would have been
more astute and clever at finding the places where
the planters had hidden their treasure.

The Negroes, inflamed by blood and a desire for
revenge, wished only to kill and burn.

"That was why you ran away from me when you

first saw me," he said, remembering the terror on her face.

"No-one had come to the house or the plantation for . . . so long," Sãona said, "that I had begun to . . . forget the danger."

"I cannot bear to think of what you have been through."

"You are . . . really the *Comte* de Villaret?" she asked, as if she was half-afraid that she had misunderstood him.

"I promise you that I am as white as you are," André said, "but when I arrived in Port-au-Prince, the friend who helped me was in fact a Mulatto. He told me it would be madness to try to reach here unless I was disguised."

"It is dangerous for you to be here now," Sãona said with a little note of fear in her voice. "There are always people watching, always someone who might betray a white man."

She looked round the garden as if she was afraid that she might see someone hiding in the bushes or the flowers.

"The Emperor has . . . spies everywhere," she added, almost beneath her breath.

"I have been lucky so far," André said reassuringly, "and whatever the reason, whatever the danger, it has been worth it to find you, my precious little love."

She raised her face to his with a look of happiness that he had never seen before, and once again he kissed her, this time possessively, demandingly.

"I love you!" he said. "I love you until it is hard to think of anything else. And now I must take you away, take you to England, my darling, to my mother."

"It will not be . . . easy," Sãona said, "and first you must have the treasure that your uncle left for you."

Because he was in love, because it was so perfect to hold Sãona in his arms, André had for the moment completely forgotten the purpose for which he had come to the plantation.

"Damballah told me that Sãona would give me the treasure," he said. "That is why I was looking for her."

"And now that . . . you have . . . found her?"

"I know I have found a treasure which is more important and more wonderful than all the money in the world."

She made a little sound of sheer happiness.

"Do you . . . really mean . . . that?"

"Are you still doubting me?" he asked.

She put her cheek against his shoulder with a movement of endearment which he knew was entirely instinctive, like a child who must touch something she loves.

"My precious, wonderful one," he said, "how soon can we get away?"

As if his words made her think again of the dangers that surrounded them, she replied:

"As soon as possible, but I am not quite certain how we can manage it."

"Leave everything to me," André said. "I will talk to Tomás, and then we will go to Le Cap and find a ship to carry us to America."

"It sounds so . . . perfect . . . so marvellous!" Sãona cried. "But supposing we are . . . caught?"

"Then we will die!" André said. "But I have a feeling, my darling, that God will protect us, our God, yours and mine, who has kept us both safely up until this moment. And also the Voodoo gods who, through their magic, spoke to me with my uncle's voice."

"You . . . heard him?"

"Although it seems incredible, and few people in England would believe me, I actually heard Uncle Philippe speaking through the lips of the *Papaloi*."

"I have heard that it happens," Sãona said, "and I can understand why the *Papaloi* wants to help you."

"Why?" André enquired.

"Because the *Comte* was always kind and understanding to those who wished to practise Voodoo. Some planters were cruel and punished their men severely if they heard the drums or thought there had been a sacrifice. But the *Comte* used to say that men cannot live without religion, and whatever god they worshipped, sooner or later it would lead them to the true God."

"That sounds like my uncle," André said. "He was a very tolerant man."

"That is why those who follow Damballah in this neighbourhood will help you," Sāona said quite seriously.

"I am very grateful," André said. "But they could not save my uncle or his family; yet perhaps they saved you."

"It was the Nuns who did that," Sāona replied, "because the *Comte* was kind to them too when they came here after the Revolution began. He gave them shelter and built them the Convent."

She gave a little sigh.

"No-one had any idea then that things were so serious, or that what was happening in the North would spread over the whole of Haiti."

"I had heard that," André said.

"The Nuns were very grateful," she went on, "and when the reports of what was occurring grew worse, they asked your uncle what they could do to help."

André knew that telling the story was distressing Sāona, but it had to be told, and he merely held her closer and his lips were on her hair as she went on:

"The *Comte* said that if his slaves revolted, which he thought was very unlikely, then the Nuns must try to save the ladies of the household, and that of course included me."

"But the others could not get away when the time came?"

"Everybody was always talking about leaving," Sāona answered. "The *Comtesse* packed a dozen times, then because everything was so peaceful and calm here, it seemed foolish to invite danger by going elsewhere."

"I can understand that," André said.

"So the *Comte* and the *Comtesse* stayed and stayed ... until one day ..."

She stopped speaking and there was a little throb in her voice.

"What happened then?"

"It was in the afternoon, and a slave came running to the house where we were sitting on the balcony, to say that a great Army was approaching on the outskirts of the plantation and setting the sugar-cane on fire."

"It must have been very frightening for you."

"I think . . . everyone was . . . frightened . . . although the *Comte* was very . . . calm and brave."

"What did you do?"

"The *Comte* said to the *Comtesse*: 'You must go at once to the Convent!' but she shook her head.

" 'I am not leaving you, Philippe,' she replied. 'My place is here at your side.'

"She then turned to the two ladies who were staying in the house.

" 'You both go,' she insisted, but they were old and they refused.

" 'If we have to die,' one of them said firmly, 'we will die with you.' "

"That is how the aristocrats behaved at the time of the Revolution in France," André said as if he spoke to himself.

"That is what we had . . . heard," Sāona replied, "but I was afraid, and I clung to the *Comtesse*. I remember thinking that I did not want to die. I wanted to live."

"You were only a child."

"I was just nine," Sāona replied. "I had celebrated my birthday the previous week."

"What happened next?" André asked.

"The *Comte* ordered an old Negress maid, who had looked after me since I had come to live in the house, to take me to the Convent."

She gave a sudden little sob as she said:

"There was . . . not even . . . time for me to say good-bye properly. 'Hurry, hurry!' the *Comte* kept saying. 'The child will be safe there, and there is no time to be lost!' "

There was a pause. Then Sāona went on, with tears in her eyes:

"I heard . . . afterwards what h-happened . . . when I had . . . gone."

"I want to know," André said, "but I do not want to upset you, my darling one."

"It is right that you should know," Sāona said. "The *Comte,* his three sons with him, waited at the front of the house, and when the men approached, screaming and yelling for vengeance, led by General Dessalines, they must have known there was no hope."

Sāona's voice was choked as she said:

"The . . . soldiers carried the . . . heads of white . . . w-women and children impaled on their . . . bayonets."

She was crying now, and André kissed her cheek and her forehead, but she still continued in a resolute little voice:

"I—I . . . heard later that . . . the *C-Comte* turned round and . . . drawing a pistol from his . . . p-pocket . . . shot the . . . *Comtesse* . . . and two of his . . . s-sons did the s-same to the other two . . . ladies! Then . . . the mob . . . killed them!"

André felt a sense of pride that his uncle and his cousins should have behaved exactly as he might have expected them to do.

He did not wish Sāona to be distressed any more, and he kissed the tears from her cheeks and her wet eyes before he kissed her lips.

"It is all over now," he said, "and you were saved."

"The soldiers began to . . . loot the Church, and the . . . Nuns ran away into the woods, with the exception of several . . . young ones who were . . . caught, and I do not . . . know what happened to them."

André had a very good idea, and he thought it was typical that Dessalines should have allowed his soldiers and those who followed him to desecrate a Church.

Both Toussaint and Christophe were good Catholics and had done their best to protect the Priests, even though they were white.

"Before he was killed," André said, "my uncle told you where he had hidden his treasure."

"I was the only ... person he told."

"Why was that?"

"He knew that many planters had been tortured and so hid their families before they died, and he therefore entrusted me with his secret, hoping that if the rebels came to the house, I should somehow be saved."

She gave him a little smile as she said:

"Perhaps he had a ... premonition. Perhaps God told him that I should be ... spared."

"I can only thank God that you were," André replied.

He kissed her again with a sudden desperation, as if he was afraid that she might be taken from him.

"I love you!" he said. "And it tortures me to think of all you have gone through."

"The Nuns have been very kind to me," Sāona told him, "but the Reverend Mother and two of the older Nuns are the only ones in the Convent who know that I am white."

"It was the Reverend Mother who thought of painting your nails and saying that you were an Octoroon?" André asked.

"She knew how fanatical General Dessalines was about the white people and she thought that it was the only way of saving me."

André looked surprised, and she said in a low voice:

"It is a temptation, even for a Nun, to curry favour by revealing the whereabouts of a white fugitive."

"I understand," he said.

"The Reverend Mother said that not even the Priests must know my secret, and so when the Priest visited us once a month, I had to hide."

André looked puzzled, and she explained:

"How could I accept Mass without having been to confession? And if I confessed, I would have had to tell the Priest."

"Of course," he said. "So all these years, my pre-

cious, you have been denied even the comfort of the
Church."

"I listened to the Services where no-one could
see me, and I prayed very hard whenever I was
alone."

"That is why I knew you were a Saint the first
time I saw you with your birds."

"I did not have to lie or have any secrets where
they were concerned," Sãona said. "It did not matter
to them what was the colour of my skin."

André kissed her again.

"We have to get away, my darling heart," he
said. "I shall never know one happy moment until I
have you safe in England. And perhaps one day, God
willing, we shall be able to go home to France, where
we both really belong."

Sãona gave a little laugh, then she said:

"I told you that my father was French. But my
mother was English."

"As mine is," André said, "and that, of course, my
lovely one, accounts for the colour of your hair."

"I am very like Mama," Sãona said, "but she was
so unhappy after Papa was killed in a battle at sea
that all she wanted to do was to join him in Heaven."

"Your father was a sailor?"

"Yes; and that was why my mother came to Haiti
in the first place, to be near him. I was born here.
But after he was killed it was impossible to get away,
and Mama was . . . so very ill."

Sãona's voice was thick with sorrow, but she fought
against the tears and after a moment she said:

"Papa had been a friend of the *Comte*, and the
moment he was told that Mama was dead, he brought
me here and said that I would be the . . . daughter he
had always . . . wanted."

"He must have loved you and been very proud
of you, as I am."

André looked at her for a long moment, then he
said:

"I want to stay here all day, telling you how much
I love you, but we have to be sensible and make
plans to get away."

"Can I really . . . go with you?" Sāona asked.

"Do you think I could leave you behind?" he enquired. "My darling, you hold all my happiness in your hands, and I swear it is true when I say that I cannot live without you."

She lifted her face to his like a flower turning its face to the sun, and he kissed her until the garden swung round them and their feet no longer were on earth and they were flying up into the sky.

Then with an almost superhuman effort André forced himself to think seriously.

"Put on your head-dress, my beautiful," he said, "so that no-one shall see your hair. Then we will go back to the house and ask Tomás to prepare the dye which will recolour our finger-nails."

Sāona picked up the white veil that André had thrown to the ground and twisted it round and round over her head.

Then once again she looked like a little white Nun, as she had been when he first saw her.

"You look very sweet," he said, "but I want to buy you silks and satins, clasp a necklace of pearls round your throat, and buy you an engagement ring that will shine as brightly as your eyes."

He smiled a little wryly.

"Unfortunately, unless you provide me with the treasure that you say my uncle left me, it will be difficult for me to buy you any of those things."

"The treasure is there," Sāona said, "but it would be wise for you to come late in the afternoon to collect it, just before dark."

"Why not after dark?" André questioned.

"Because we should need lights, and if anyone saw lights in the Church, they might come to investigate."

"The treasure is in the Church?"

She nodded.

"My uncle said in a letter to my father," André told her, "that he had put it in the earth and in the shadow of God."

"That is exactly what he did," Sāona said, "and I will show you where to find it."

"Thank you, my darling," André said. "Now, let us attend to our hands, and then I will take you back."

"The Reverend Mother will wonder what has happened to me," Sāona said with a smile, "but I often stay in the woods for a long time."

"You must be careful, very careful," André warned quickly. "I might, after all, have been a Mulatto who would have hurt you."

"When I . . . talked to you in the Church . . . I knew that despite my fears, you would never . . . hurt me."

"How did you know that?" André enquired.

"I think it must have been love that told me," she said simply.

He kissed her again, then they returned to the front of the house and climbed the steps.

Tomás was waiting for them, and as soon as André smelt the aroma of the bowl he held in his hand, he knew he had already boiled the dye with which to stain their fingers.

The Negro was smiling broadly and André said:

"You are an old fox, Tomás! How did you know that *Mademoiselle* Sāona's disguise was as false as mine?"

"Damballah promise find *M'mselle*," Tomás replied.

"I suppose that is as near as we shall ever get to the truth," André said quietly to Sāona. "But it will keep me puzzling for years as to whether Tomás guessed that you were not what you pretended to be, or heard a rumour in the village, or whether it was in fact the drums and Damballah himself who told him the truth."

"As you say, we shall never know," Sāona replied, "but he was clever enough to tell me the truth about you."

"It was something he had no right to do!" André retorted, but he was smiling as he spoke.

Tomás painted quite skilfully the half-moons of Sāona's fingers, then restored the brown to André's.

"I had no idea that it was so easy to remove this dye," he said.

"One tree make brown, other tree make white," Tomás explained. "White tree very secret. Few people know."

"There are all too many secrets in Haiti," André said. "At the same time, Tomás, if the white tree grows here, please bring plenty of it with us when we leave."

Tomás nodded, as if he had already thought that this would be necessary.

"I must go now," Sāona said, looking at her nails to see if they were dry.

"I will walk back with you through the wood," André said.

They moved towards the window, then he stopped.

"Tomás," he said, "we must all three of us get to Le Cap as soon as possible. We shall need another horse."

"Not difficult," Tomás replied.

"It will have to be a good one," André said, "and it would be wisest to say that one of our animals has gone lame. Otherwise it might seem strange that though there are only two of us, we should require three horses."

Tomás nodded again, and André, holding Sāona by the hand, left the house and they climbed the path which led through the wood.

While they went, she told him of how charming the Habitation de Villaret had been before it had been destroyed and burnt.

André had not seen his uncle and aunt for many years, but, listening to Sāona's description of them and the manner in which they had lived, he felt as if they came alive for him.

Their three sons had been fine young men, interested in the plantation, and the youngest one had been, Sāona said, a clever artist.

"It was thinking of his pictures," she said, "which made me suggest that we might decorate the chancel of the Church."

"It was your idea?" André asked.

"I found that Sister Térèsa loved drawing and

painting, and as you have seen, she is very clever at it."

"I thought the murals, although they were primitive, had a strange beauty about them."

"I thought that too," Sāona said, "and they were painted with loving care, which I am sure helps."

"I am sure it does," André agreed.

He thought she herself exuded those two virtues, love and faith, and it was hard to believe that there was any woman in the world who, living the life she had lived, could have remained so beautiful, not only in her face but in her personality and in her very soul.

He thought, when he left her after they had kissed for a very long time in the shade of a frangipani tree, that he was in fact the most fortunate of all men.

"I will come to the Church," he said, "at about four o'clock. I will be there praying until you think it safe to join me."

"You will . . . really pray?" she asked him.

"I have a great deal of thanksgiving to give," he replied, "and a great many favours to ask for the immediate future."

She gave a little sigh.

"I will say many, many novenas that we may arrive safely."

"I cannot believe that your prayers will not be answered," André said, and he meant it in all sincerity.

*   *   *

When he was back at the house, he thought how strange everything was and how in fact he had been incredibly lucky, not only in reaching the Habitation de Villaret without any difficulty but also in finding the girl he sought.

He could only hope that his uncle's treasure, which he had hidden so sensibly, would be enough for the two of them in the future.

One thing which worried him, but which he had not confided to Sāona, was that if the treasure was at all bulky, it would not only be difficult to take it to Le Cap but it might also prove extremely dangerous.

Heavy bags that might contain money were always suspect in times of unrest, and gold was not a commodity that was easy to convey from one place to another, unless there was an insignificant amount of it.

'I shall have to think of some way of disguising what we carry,' André thought.

He told himself that it would be difficult to have a really constructive idea until he saw the actual bulk of what his uncle had buried.

When he reached the Habitation de Villaret there was no sign of Tomás or of any midday meal, and André realised he was in fact extremely hungry.

All the emotions that he had passed through since this morning had, he thought, in some way drained his strength, and yet he could never remember a time in his life when he had been happier or more content within himself.

He had always laughed at the idea of love at first sight, and at men who claimed that their whole life had been changed from the moment they met some particular woman.

And yet that was exactly what had happened to him, and now it was impossible to translate what had occurred into the confinement of ordinary time.

He did not feel as if he had known Sāona for two days, but for two million years. She was there in his heart and soul.

She was his, completely and absolutely, as if they had been married for half a lifetime.

He knew their thoughts were in unison, their hearts beat to a strange rhythm that made them one, and their souls were united, as Sāona would have said, by the blessing of God.

André looked out into the beauty of the garden, then raised his eyes to the sky.

"*Merci, mon Dieu!*" he said aloud.

It was the most sincere and heartfelt prayer he had ever made.

Tomás returned a little while later to say that he had found exactly the kind of horse they wanted and in fact it was not too expensive. If André would give him the money he would fetch it that very afternoon.

"The sooner the better!" André said. "I have now found everything I sought, Tomás, and we must be on our way."

"Buy horse, then go," Tomás said.

"I will tell *Mademoiselle* to be ready tomorrow morning," André replied. "You know the way to Le Cap?"

Tomás nodded again.

He never wasted words. Then he went to fetch André another glass of the fruit-juice which he kept cool in the well.

Luncheon was so late that André had very little time to waste before he need set off for the Church.

He debated with himself whether he would go on horse-back or whether he would walk.

If he rode he could, he thought, bring back to the house some of the treasure that was waiting for him.

On the other hand, he would have to leave the horse in the usual place outside the Church, and it might arouse some curiosity.

He had seen very few people since he had come to the Habitation de Villaret, but he was well aware that there were small villages scattered over the plantation and men working amongst the sugar-canes and the banana-groves in their own interests.

It was inevitable that they should be curious about a stranger, and André thought that this was a moment when it would be extremely unwise to draw attention to himself.

"I will walk," he decided, "then later, perhaps very early tomorrow morning, when it is light, Tomás and I can come back together to move anything that is too heavy for me to carry alone!"

He reached the Church a little after four o'clock, and, entering through the west door, which as usual was open, he knelt down to pray.

It was very quiet and cool inside the old Church and he wondered how many people through the ages had brought their troubles, their difficulties, and their problems to lay them at the feet of God, feeling sure that He would help them.

André knew that if before he had been apprehensive about his own safety, every anxiety now would be doubled by his fear for Sāona.

It seemed incredible that in her short life she should have already passed through so much unhappiness and so much sheer agonising terror.

Yet he could understand that it had deepened her personality and character and made her in some ways very much older than she would have been had she lived in normal circumstances.

It had also given her an awareness and a sensitivity that he had never found in any other woman.

He was thinking so deeply about her that she reached his side without his being aware of it, and only when she touched his shoulder did he rise from his knees.

He looked into her face and thought that the love in her eyes and the faint smile that touched her lips gave her a radiance to which his whole being responded.

She did not speak, and he raised her hand and kissed it.

She turned from him to shut the door and put a wooden bolt across it. Then, slipping her hand into his, she led him up the aisle.

They both genuflected before the altar with its wooden cross and André glanced up for a moment at the murals which decorated the walls.

He felt as if the colour and the strange beauty of the paintings gave him a feeling of protection and understanding.

He could not explain the feeling to himself, and yet it was there.

Sāona was drawing him and now they went behind the altar to walk down two stone steps to a lower level.

The altar had been built out from the east wall
of the Church so that one could pass behind it, but
the space was narrow and flagged with heavy stones.

Sãona went forward and stopped directly oppo-
site the centre of the altar.

There were flowers and candles at head level
and soaring above them was the roughly carved
wooden cross which André had noticed the first time
he had come to the Church.

Sãona glanced up; then, bending down, she
pointed with her finger to a large, flat square stone
placed directly behind the altar, which was, André
realised with a leap of his heart, in the shadow of the
cross!

He knew she wished him to lift the stone, and
was wondering how to do so when from beneath the
altar itself she produced an iron crowbar and a small
trowel.

She handed him the crowbar, and it was not difficult to insert it beneath the stone, and by exerting
only a small amount of strength he lifted it quite
easily.

Once it was raised at one side, André lifted it
with his hands.

He looked and saw that there was only earth
beneath it, but the aperture was quite small and he
thought with some dismay that anything that was
hidden there would not be very big.

But Sãona smiled at him encouragingly and
handed him the trowel.

Kneeling down and holding it in his hand, he
began to dig into the heavy earth.

He went down about a foot in depth, then
struck something.

He put his hand into the hole and drew out a
leather bag which was not very big but jingled when
he moved it.

Now it was hard not to express not only his dis-
appointment but also his dismay.

There could not be very much money in such a
small bag, and he was certain, in fact, that the louis

would not amount to more than a few thousand francs.

Without even bothering to open the bag he set it at his side, and looking at Sāona he asked:

"Shall I put the soil back?"

She smiled at him as if he were a child who was being rather stupid.

"Dig deeper," she said in a whisper. "That is there only as a blind to make thieves think that was all they would find."

"There is more?" André asked, with a new light in his eyes.

"You will see," she answered.

He dug with a new energy and now he had to go down very much deeper, and the pile of soil beside him grew and grew.

Then once again the trowel struck something, and he had to insert almost the whole length of his arm to grasp yet another leather bag.

It was a little larger than the other one, but not much, and once again his spirits fell.

He looked at Sāona, thinking perhaps he had to dig deeper still, but now she said softly:

"Look inside."

The bag was tightly tied but he undid it, thinking as he did so that it was not very heavy and the louis, if that was what it contained, would not be very valuable.

The bag opened and he looked inside.

For a moment he could not understand what he saw. Then in the light that came from a window over their heads, something glistened.

He gave a little exclamation and put his hand into the bag.

"Diamonds!" he said, and there was no mistaking the astonishment in his voice.

"Yes, diamonds," Sāona whispered. "When your uncle showed me where he had hidden them, he told me he had been buying them for a long time, knowing they would be more easy to carry if he had to leave the country in a hurry."

"Diamonds!" André repeated beneath his breath.

Some of the stones were large, very large, and some were small, but as he touched them they seemed to glitter almost like imprisoned sunshine, and he knew that each one was extremely valuable and that the whole collection was worth a very great fortune.

He saw at once how much cleverer his uncle had been than the other planters whose wealth was in gold and silver plate, the loot that Dessalines had carried back to Port-au-Prince on twenty-five donkeys.

This fortune, and he was quite certain it was a very considerable one, would require no effort to take away, only constant surveillance for fear that it might be stolen.

As if the value of it already made him conscious that he must be extremely careful, André handed the bag of diamonds to Sāona and hastily pushed the soil back into the hole from which it had come.

He was careful not to leave any earth behind before he replaced the heavy stone that had guarded it so well.

Then he picked up the other bag that contained the gold and they walked from behind the altar back into the chancel.

Once again they both genuflected, then walked silently towards the bolted door.

Only as they reached it did André say in a low voice:

"How can I thank you?"

"Thank God, who protected it for you for so long."

"I will do that," he said. "And will you be ready early tomorrow morning to leave with me?"

"I have already told the Reverend Mother. She understands," Sāona answered. "She is giving me an address in Le Cap where we will be safe until we can find a ship."

"Will you thank her?" André asked.

"I have already done so," Sāona answered. "But if you see her tomorrow, do not mention what we have found here."

"I would not have thought of doing so," André

replied. "I understand it has been in your special care, and because my uncle trusted you, I know you would not have mentioned it to anyone."

"No-one," Sāona agreed, "but sometimes I wondered what would happen if I should grow old and die and no De Villaret came to claim it."

"Fortunately, that did not happen," André said, "and now, my darling, we can share it in the future, and you will be able to have all the things I want to give you."

Her face was very lovely as she lifted her lips to his.

"I only want . . . you," she whispered.

*   *   *

Back in the house later that night, André sat on his bed and looked at the bag of diamonds, trying to estimate their value.

He had little knowledge of stones. His mother had only a few jewels left of the very valuable collection she had owned before the French Revolution.

There was one ring in particular which she had refused to sell, however hard up they might be, because she said she was keeping it for his wife.

"It has been in the family for two hundred years," she said. "I cannot bear to think that we should turn it into anything so mundane as bread because we are hungry!"

"It could provide us with far more delectable things to eat than bread!" André had laughed.

"I know that," his mother replied, "in fact, I was offered a thousand pounds for this ring by a jeweller in Bond Street when I went to have the setting repaired."

"A thousand pounds!" André had exclaimed.

"That is the settlement for your wife," his mother had said. "You will have little else to offer her, and I would not wish you to approach any woman completely empty-handed."

André understood the sacrifice she was making on his behalf, and he kissed her.

"Thank you," he said, "but if you ever really need money for yourself, I shall insist upon you selling it."

The diamonds in his mother's ring did not compare with many of the gems in the bag.

'I am rich!' he thought.

Then he knew that what really made him a wealthy man was the love and possession of Sāona.

"Please, God, let us reach England in safety," he prayed before he went to sleep.

The two bags were close to him as he closed his eyes.

* * *

André was awakened suddenly by Tomás shaking his arm, and he opened his eyes, bewildered at being awakened from what had been a deep and dreamless sleep.

"Wake, *M'sieur*, wake!" Tomás was saying urgently.

André sat up.

"What is it, Tomás?"

"Leave now—quickly!"

"Why?"

"Drums tell soldiers come from Port-au-Prince!"

"Soldiers?" André asked quickly.

"Soldiers seek *M'sieur*."

André rose from the bed and put on his clothes.

He had been a fool, he thought, not to have anticipated that this might happen.

Orchis had known that he was coming here to search for the treasure which Dessalines had not found, and she was sending soldiers to make certain that she profited by his discovery.

What mattered now was how much time he and Sāona had in which to get away before they would be apprehended, searched, and doubtless killed.

He did not even bother to ask how the drums should know that he was being threatened. It was enough to have been warned, enough to know that he had a chance, at any rate, of getting Sāona to safety.

He pulled on his boots, picked up the two bags that lay on his bed, and, carrying them, hurried outside to where Tomás was already waiting with the three horses, his clothes strapped to their saddles.

André took the reins from him and handed him the bags of gold.

"Put this one in your bundle, Tomás," he ordered, "and the other in mine."

Tomás did so with surprising swiftness.

Then, without wasting any words, André mounted and Tomás followed him, leading the extra horse as they rode down the drive.

Chapter Seven

They reached the Convent by the light of the stars and the pale moon, which was rising.

Everything was still and quiet and the moonlight gleamed on the brass bell which hung over the Convent door.

André dismounted and, giving the reins of his horse to Tomás, put his hand towards the bell, then changed his mind.

He thought a bell ringing out in the night might attract undesirable attention. Instead, he knocked on the door sharply, and after waiting for a moment knocked again.

Surprisingly quickly the door was opened, and a very old Nun peered out into the darkness.

"Who is it?" she asked in a quavering voice.

"I have to see Sister Dévotée and the Reverend Mother immediately!" André replied. "But there is no need for anyone to be frightened."

"Sister Dévotée?" the Nun repeated, as if she did not hear very well.

"And the Reverend Mother," André finished, raising his voice a little.

The Nun made as if to shut the door, but before she could do so André stepped inside.

She looked at him uncertainly, and he said gently but in an authoritative tone:

"Please fetch the Reverend Mother immediately and awaken Sister Dévotée."

The Nun shuffled away, her footsteps scraping over the flagged floor.

André waited impatiently, recognising the atmosphere of the Convent to be one of cleanliness and sanctity.

He was well aware that every second was of importance and he could only think how fortunate he was that the Voodoo drums had warned them in time to give him and Sāona a chance to escape.

There was the sound of footsteps, and looking towards the shadows at the end of the passage, he saw, with a sense of relief, the Reverend Mother coming towards him.

She was fully dressed and he thought that she had been keeping a midnight vigil of prayer, so there had been no need to awaken her.

She came quickly, considering her age, and as she reached him she said before he could speak:

"There is danger?"

André nodded.

"The Voodoo drums told my man-servant that soldiers have been sent in search of me."

"Then you must get away immediately!" the Reverend Mother said in a brisk tone of voice.

"I will take Sāona to safety in England," André said.

"That is what she told me."

The Reverend Mother hesitated for a moment, then she said:

"She also told me that you love each other."

"As soon as possible she will become my wife."

André saw the gladness in the old woman's face and he said:

"Thank you for looking after her and protecting her. I know that without you she would have died."

"Your uncle died bravely, as did all his family," the Reverend Mother said.

"Sāona told you who I am?" André enquired.

"Yes, and I am glad that you should take Sāona away. There is no life for her here and there is the danger that one day she might be discovered."

"You are very understanding," André said.

There was the sound of running feet and a moment later Sãona joined them.

André looked up eagerly as she appeared, only to be stunned for a moment into silence.

As if she knew what he was feeling, the Reverend Mother said gently:

"It is a wise precaution. It would be dangerous, very dangerous, for any woman who appeared to be white to go to Le Cap at the moment."

André understood only too well why she had disguised Sãona. At the same time, it was a shock.

Instead of her white, almost translucent skin, which was so much a part of her beauty, her face and hands were as brown as his.

What was more, she was wearing the wimple and black veil of a Nun such as the Reverend Mother wore.

For a moment André was almost shocked that anyone as beautiful as Sãona should appear so changed. Then he saw a pleading expression in her eyes, as if she asked him to understand, and he smiled as he said:

"You still look very lovely, my darling, but I shall have to be careful what I say to you in that habit!"

He knew that the lightness with which he spoke relieved Sãona's anxiety.

Then the Reverend Mother said:

"You must waste no more time. Here is a letter for you to carry to my brother; he is a Priest at the Church of Our Lady at Le Cap. Go to him and ask his help, but do not tell him that you are not what you appear to be."

The Reverend Mother gave a little sigh, then added:

"I feel sure he would not betray you; at the same time, it is best for him not to be involved."

"You are very wise," André said, "and thank you again for all you have done for my future wife."

He took the old Nun's hand as he spoke and

raised it to his lips. Then Sāona went down on her knees in front of her.

"André has thanked you, but my heart is too full. All I ask is your blessing before I leave you and go out into the world, which will be very strange and sometimes frightening because you will not be there to guide me."

André saw the tears come into the Reverend Mother's eyes. Then she said:

"God has blessed you, my child, as He has blessed the man you love, and His protection will be with you wherever you may go."

Her voice broke on the words, and Sāona rose to her feet and kissed her on each cheek.

Then she turned to André and he took her by the hand and led her out of the Convent to where Tomás was waiting outside.

He lifted her up onto the saddle, and then, without speaking, without looking back, they rode off, Tomás going ahead to guide their way.

They rode until the sun had risen and it grew very hot.

Then because they were hungry and thirsty they sat down in the shade of a tree near a cascade which fell in a silver torrent down the side of a mountain.

"How long will it take us to get to Le Cap?" Sāona asked as Tomás brought them food from his saddle-bag and a bottle of the fruit-juices he had blended so delectably.

"I have no idea," André answered. "It will depend on how quickly we can travel."

"We seem to have gone a long way already."

"Are you very stiff, my darling?" André asked. "It has been a hard ride for one who is not used to riding a horse."

"I used to ride every day, when I lived with your uncle, but now I am out of practice and I am afraid I shall be stiff, but it is unimportant."

"Nothing that concerns you is unimportant," André replied.

She turned her face aside because he was looking at her.

"I do not . . . like you to . . . see me . . . like
this," she murmured.

"You still look very beautiful to me," he said,
"but I am rather over-awed by the dark veil."

"But you know I am a fraud," Sãona said with a
smile. "Only no-one else must know."

"The Reverend Mother was very sensible," André said. "It would have been impossible for you, who
are so beautiful, to be kept safe in any place where
other men could see you."

"I want you to think me beautiful," Sãona said,
"but you do . . . understand that I am very . . .
ignorant of any life except that which I have lived
for the past ten years in the Convent with the Nuns."

She gave him a shy little glance, then went
on:

"Perhaps when you know me better you will find
me . . . boring. I may make many . . . mistakes."

"I shall never find you anything but the most
adorable and the most interesting person I have ever
known in my life," André said. "It is not only what
you say and think which intrigues me, my darling,
but what you are, which vibrates from you like a
magical aura."

"You make me so happy," Sãona said. "While I
was getting ready to come with you today, I kept
asking myself whether it was fair for you to be sad-
dled with a woman who really comes from another
world."

"You are going to live in my world in the future,"
André replied, "a world, darling, where all that matters
is that we shall be together."

He put out his hand to touch hers, then Tomás
was beside them, collecting the remains of the food
they had been eating and the bottle that contained
the fruit-juice.

"Go on, *M'sieur!*" he said firmly.

"You are worse than a slave-driver!" André complained, and Tomás grinned.

There was no doubt that he was anxious for them to be on their way and André knew he was right.

They were all very tired before Tomás found a suitable place for them to spend the night.

This time there was no question of finding an empty *Caille* or asking the protection of villagers.

André understood without being told that the fewer people who saw them, the safer it would be.

When the soldiers did not find him at the Habitation de Villaret, they would undoubtedly guess that he was on his way to Le Cap.

He hoped it would never enter anybody's mind that a woman was accompanying him.

At the same time, he had already been told a hundred times that it was impossible in Haiti for anything to remain a secret for long.

Tomás found them a place under the trees at the foot of a mountain.

André thought he might have guessed that Tomás would avoid the forest, of which he was afraid. But the place he had chosen was well hidden, and the ground was soft and mossy and not too overgrown with vegetation.

Tomás provided Sāona and André with a blanket each. Then, after they had eaten, they lay down side by side, while the Negro vanished into the darkness.

The horses were tethered a little way away from them and they were alone.

"I want to kiss you, my darling," André said, putting out his hand to find hers.

"No."

"No?" he questioned.

"I do not wish you to . . . kiss me when I . . . look like this. It might . . . spoil it."

He smiled at the almost childish note in her voice and said:

"To touch your lips will always be an experience so wonderful that it would be impossible for me to describe it in words, but if you would rather wait, then I will do anything you wish."

His fingers held hers very tightly and he said:

"I understand what you are feeling. All I want you to know is that I love you so overwhelmingly that I would never do anything to hurt or upset you."

"You . . . are so . . . wonderful!" Sāona said with a little throb in her voice. "And one day perhaps I will be able to tell you how much I . . . love you."

André did not answer for a moment. He felt he had so much to say, so much love to express, and yet somehow there was no need to put what he felt into words.

They belonged to each other, and whatever was happening, whatever they looked like, they still belonged. Even when they were married, he thought, it would be hard to be closer spiritually than they were at this moment.

He felt her fingers relaxing in his and a few seconds later he knew that she was asleep.

He too was tired, but before he slept he dedicated himself to look after and protect her, even as a Knight of old might have done when he knelt all night in the Chapel in prayer before he set out to prove his Knighthood.

They were both still fast asleep when Tomás woke them.

Then they were off again, another day of riding quickly in the morning, when the air was comparatively cool, until as it grew hot, the horses slowed their pace.

André even found it hard at times not to fall asleep in the saddle.

The way to Le Cap was easier and far less mountainous than the ride had been from Port-au-Prince.

They were, in fact, covering the miles with a speed that André knew pleased Tomás and made him hope that they would arrive in the Port quicker than he had anticipated.

The next night they were in the plains, where the ground was cultivated and it was difficult to know where it would be safe to sleep.

Tomás eventually found a place, and although the

trees were not so high or so protective, and there
were villagers not far away, André thought it would
be reasonably safe.

Tomás had ridden away from them when they
stopped at midday to buy food.

It was not very appetising, but, combined with
the fruit which grew wild everywhere, it was enough
to satisfy their hunger.

Once again André and Sāona slept almost as
soon as they lay down on their blankets.

He had in fact for the last few hours of the day
been worried about Sāona, even though she never
complained.

He thought at times she sagged a little in the
saddle, and he wondered if he should suggest that she
ride with him, so that he could hold her in his arms.

Then he knew it was a risk they dare not take.

What could look stranger than a Nun riding with
a man on his horse and being held close against his
heart?

"There will only be one more night," André told
himself reassuringly, "then we shall reach Le Cap."

He drifted away into a tired dream, to wake with
a start to find Tomás kneeling beside him.

"What is it?" he asked.

"Move on, M'sieur!"

"Now?" André asked, realising it was still the
middle of the night.

"Drums warn danger!"

"The drums?" André asked.

Even as he said the words, he heard them far
away in the distance, so far they might have been
little more than the beating of his heart, and yet
they were there.

"What are they saying?" he asked.

"Danger for you, M'sieur."

"Me? Are you telling me that your Voodoo
friends in this part of the world know who I am?"

"Damballah protect, M'sieur."

There was almost a rebuke in Tomás's voice and
André got to his feet.

"I am already deeply in Damballah's debt," he

said. "If he says we must move on, we will follow his instructions."

He bent over Sāona.

"Wake up, darling," he said. "We have to be on our way."

She opened her eyes and shut them again.

"I am . . . so . . . tired."

"I know, my precious," André said, "but the drums are warning us of danger."

She stiffened at the word.

"D-danger?"

"So Tomás tells us," André said. "Do you hear them?"

She sat up.

"I can hear . . . them."

"Then we must do what they tell us," André told her.

He helped her to her feet, Tomás collected the blankets and tied them to the saddle of one of the horses, and then they were off once again.

They rode for nearly two hours before the moon and the stars faded, and an incredibly beautiful dawn crept up the sky, golden with promise.

Because they had made such an early start to the day, André was not surprised when as they stopped to eat Tomás said:

"Reach Le Cap tonight."

André looked at Sāona anxiously.

"Are you strong enough to do it?" he asked. "It would be best, I am quite certain, to arrive when it is dark."

"I shall be . . . all right," Sāona said briefly.

He could see by her eyes how tired she was.

"I suppose there is no chance of us getting a little brandy or some wine?" he asked Tomás.

"I find, *M'sieur*," the Negro answered.

A few miles farther on, he told them to wait for him while he rode into a nearby village.

When he came back he had a black bottle that André knew before they opened it, was Clarin.

He remembered only too vividly where he had

seen the same bottle before: at the Voodoo ceremony
when the *Papaloi* and the *Mamaloi* had drunk deeply, then blown the rum out in white clouds towards
the other participants in the ceremony.

André tasted it and realised it was very strong.
At the same time, it warmed him inside and would,
he knew, take away the feeling of tension and relieve
sheer exhaustion.

He told Tomás to get out the cup that he carried
in his saddle-bag. He filled it half-full with the juice
of an orange, which he had picked from a tree, and
added some rum.

"Drink this, darling," he said to Sãona.

"Is it safe to do so?" she asked. "Supposing I fall
off my horse?"

"You will not do that," André said, "and it will
make you feel a little stronger."

She drank it because she knew he wished her to
do so, then he drank some more himself and insisted
that Tomás did the same.

Three hours later they stopped for another drink,
and by now André was certain that the Clarin was
the only thing that was keeping Sãona going.

She was so tired that she could no longer speak,
and when they rode on just after the sun had sunk, he
reached out to take the reins of her horse from her,
so that he could lead it.

"Hold on with both your hands, my precious," he
said. "We really have not much farther to go now."

He was speaking optimistically, but half-an-hour
later he saw the lights of Le Cap ahead and in the
great bay in front of the town the lights of several
ships.

It was impossible to know what kind they were
or of what nationality He could only pray with a
fervour that came from sheer desperation that one
of them would be American.

He had a feeling that Tomás had been more
perturbed by the message of the drums than he
would admit.

More than once during the day, as they rode as

quickly as the horses could carry them, he had noticed that Tomás looked back, almost as if he was expecting to see soldiers following them.

But now Le Cap lay ahead, and the lights from the houses were more welcome than any lights André had ever seen in his life before.

They clattered through the narrow streets, which even at this time of the night seemed filled with people.

There were soldiers off-duty, seated on doorsteps with their arms round Negro girls.

Vendors of food and other commodities were plying their wares to anyone who would listen to them.

Quite a number of men, the majority of them soldiers, seemed to be the worse for drink.

André thought it was typical of an Army that had had very little training and which, he had heard, showed an ever-increasing disinclination to obey their Officers.

Tomás obviously knew the way and they hurried through the streets, few people paying any attention to them except to look occasionally with surprise at seeing a Nun on horse-back.

Then André saw the spire of a Church silhouetted against the stars, and as Tomás brought his tired horse to a standstill he knew they had arrived.

He dismounted and lifted Sāona from her horse, only to find, as he tried to put her down on the ground, that she was too tired to stand.

Instead, he picked her up in his arms again and Tomás went to the door of the wooden house next to the Church and knocked on it.

With Sāona in his arms, her head resting on his shoulder, André waited, thinking as he did so that the first thing he must do was to remove the bundles from the back of the saddles, which contained the gold and the diamonds.

As if Tomás read his thoughts, the Negro turned to say:

"Fetch now, *M'sieur*."

"Do that," André said, and moved nearer to the door.

It opened and he saw a man dressed in a cassock looking out at him.

He was a Negro and André knew that this must be the Reverend Mother's brother.

"Who are you and what do you want?" the Priest enquired.

"I have a letter from your sister, *mon Père*," André answered. "She thought you would be kind enough to find somewhere for us to rest. We have ridden a long way."

"My sister?" the Priest exclaimed in surprise. Then he added quickly:

"Come in, my son! Is that one of my sister's Nuns you have with you?"

"She is very tired," André answered.

The Priest led the way into the house, which was small and very sparsely furnished.

André put Sāona gently down on a chair. Her eyes were closed and she looked completely exhausted.

"I was just having something to eat," the Priest said. "I wonder if you would join me—the coffee is hot."

"Coffee would be more welcome than anything else," André answered. "We are also hungry."

"You are welcome to anything I have," the Priest replied.

As he spoke, Tomás came in with the rolled bundles that had been attached to the saddles and set them down just inside the door.

"You will find a place at the back to put the horses," the Priest said to him.

"I will help him," André said, and walking from the room followed Tomás out into the night.

"Stable the horses, then try to find out if there is an American ship in the Harbour," he said in a low voice.

Tomás did not answer, and André knew he would do what he was asked.

Not liking to leave Sāona for long, André went back into the house and shut the door behind him.

He found the Priest handing her a cup of coffee, and although it was an effort, she managed to raise it to her lips.

André also accepted one from the Priest.

It was thick and black, but because he was so tired and thirsty, he thought that it was the best coffee he had ever tasted.

He felt his tiredness ebbing away from him and knew that Sāona was feeling the same.

"You must stay here the night," the Priest said, "and tomorrow you must tell me how I can assist you."

"I think the Reverend Mother will have explained a great deal in this letter," André said, taking it from the inner pocket of his coat.

"When you left her, she was well and—safe?"

There was a pause between the last words, which told André that the Priest had been worried about his sister.

"She was quite safe," he said, "and she helped us to get away."

"Get away?" the Priest questioned sharply.

"She knew that soldiers were coming from Port-au-Prince to look for me."

The Priest's lips tightened, then he said:

"The Emperor is on his way here. He should arrive sometime tomorrow!"

"What has happened?" André asked.

"His expedition against the Spanish was not successful."

"That, I imagine, will not put him in a particularly good temper!" André said. "And as you well know, *mon Père*, he does not like Mulattos."

"Then you would be wise to leave," the Priest said.

"We shall try to do so," André replied, "but I have a favour to ask of you first."

"What is it?" the Priest enquired.

"The lady with me is not a Nun," André replied.

"She is a young girl whom your sister has sheltered and looked after for ten years. I would ask you to marry us."

The Priest looked surprised. Then he said:

"If you are to leave Le Cap before the Emperor arrives, then I had better marry you this evening."

"That is what I hoped you would agree to do," André replied.

Sāona was sitting up, staring at him with astonishment.

He went to her, took the empty cup and saucer from her hands, and said quietly:

"Why should we wait any longer to be man and wife?"

He looked into her eyes as he spoke and saw an expression of love and trust which made his heart turn over in his breast.

"I will do ... whatever you ... wish," she whispered.

He raised her hand and kissed it.

"I expect you would like to freshen yourselves up," the Priest said. "When you are ready, come through that door, which will take you straight into the Church. I will be waiting for you."

"Thank you, *mon Père*," André answered.

"It will not be possible tonight," the Priest went on, "to perform the Nuptial Mass, but you can attend the Service that I shall be taking anyway at seven o'clock tomorrow morning, and I can hear your confessions at six forty-five."

He did not wait for their reply, but went through the door that opened into the Church.

André drew Sāona to her feet.

"I know you have a lot of questions to ask, my precious one," he said, "and perhaps you think I am being unduly hasty. But I have the inescapable feeling that we must not miss this opportunity, and tomorrow, one way or another, we must get away from Le Cap."

"I ... understand," Sāona said. "I am happy to do ... anything you want."

André kissed her hand again.

"I think that as this house seems very small," Sāona went on, "it will not be difficult to find somewhere where I can wash at least some of the dust from my face."

There was a door leading out of the room and André guessed it would be the Priest's bed-room.

There was a basin of water in one corner, and he carried in one of the lamps from the Sitting-Room so that Sāona could see what she was doing.

Then, because he had an idea of how the wooden houses were constructed, he went out through what was obviously the back door and found himself in a small courtyard.

As he had expected, there was a well, and he pumped some water over his head, washed his hands, and felt cooler and cleaner.

He wished he could change out of his dusty clothes for such an important occasion as his marriage, and he knew that Sāona, being a woman, would be wishing that she could be wearing the traditional white wedding-gown with a lace veil and a wreath of orange-blossoms.

"Nothing matters," he told himself, "except that she should be my wife."

He went back into the Sitting-Room and undid the bundles that Tomás had put just inside the door.

It suddenly struck him that it was dangerous to have all the diamonds in one bag which he could not even carry with him.

Quickly, before Sāona returned, he opened the bag and filled his pockets with some of the gems.

Then because the bag was still half-full he undid the lining of his coat and tipped them inside.

He thought, as he did so, that he must be careful not to pull off his coat and fling it down to release a shower of diamonds, which would be surprising to say the very least of it.

The bag that had contained the diamonds was empty and he put it back with his clothes, then picked up the bag of gold.

This, he thought, would doubtless prove very useful, for the money he had brought with him to Haiti had been heavily depleted.

He set a number of guineas aside as a present for Tomás, then wrapped the bag up with his clothes and tied it neatly as it had been before.

The third roll, which had been attached to the saddle of Sãona's horse, was hers and he knew she would need it when the Priest told them where they would be able to sleep tonight.

There was a staircase, rather narrow and rickety, which led to an upper floor and he supposed that was where the rooms were that they would occupy.

He had only just finished tying a fresh cravat round his neck when Sãona came back into the room.

She was still wearing the long veil and wimple, but he thought she looked fresher and her eyes were shining in a way which told him she was excited.

She ran towards him and put her hands against his chest.

"Are we . . . really to be . . . married tonight?" she asked. "I thought perhaps I was . . . dreaming when you told me we were."

"You were not dreaming, my precious one," he said. "I want above everything else to know that you are my wife, before we begin to make plans for the future."

"The . . . Emperor is coming here . . . tomorrow."

"I know," he said, "but have you forgotten that we are both specially protected people?"

She smiled up at him and he resisted an impulse to kiss her.

He longed for the feel of her lips beneath his and to make her quiver in his arms as she had done when he kissed her in the garden.

There would be time for that later, if God was merciful and allowed them to escape from what he felt at the back of his mind was a trap that was gradually closing in on them.

"Come," he said. "We must be married, my lovely one, and that is very much more important to me than anything else."

He took her by the hand and they went through
the door at the side which the Priest had told them
led to the Church.

It was a very small Church, built after the fire
which had devastated every building at Le Cap, and
was roughly constructed of wood. But all the familiar
signs and symbols were there—the Stations of the
Cross, the statues of Our Lady and St. Anthony, and
the sanctuary lamp gleaming red above the altar on
which burnt six candles.

The Priest was waiting for them, a prayer-book
in his hand, and André led Sāona forward to kneel in
front of him.

The Service was the same as if they had been in
the Cathedral of Nôtre Dame or of Chartres, and the
beautiful prayers which they had both known since
they were children seemed to have a special significance for them.

It suddenly struck André how strange it was that
he, who had always resisted the idea of marriage,
should be united with a girl he had met only a few
days ago.

He was being married to her when both their
skins were dyed in order to disguise them as Mulattos, and his bride was wearing the borrowed gar-
ments of a Nun.

But he knew as the Priest joined them together
and he repeated the age-old vows of the Marriage
Service that how they appeared was of no consequence.

It was their hearts beating as one, and their
souls united in dedicating themselves not only to
each other but to the God they both worshipped, that
mattered.

The Priest raised his hands and the words of the
blessing seemed to come from his lips almost as if
he was inspired:

*"Dominus Deus Omnipotens benedicat vos, im-
pleat que benedictionem in vobis."*

"Amen!" André said in his heart, and heard
Sāona's "Amen," very soft and little above a whisper.

Suddenly a voice rang out from the end of the Church:

"*M'sieur! M'sieur!*"

André turned his head, then started to his feet.

It was Tomás who stood there, shouting breathlessly:

"Come! Come quick! Boat waiting. Quick!"

"There is a ship?" André questioned.

"American ship leaving. Come!"

André pulled Sāona to her feet.

"*Merci, mon Père,*" he said, and ran not towards the end of the Church but through the door that led into the Priest's room.

He snatched up the bundles; then, pulling open the door into the street, he hurried out to find that Tomás, aware of what he was doing, had run round to the Church door to meet them.

He took the bundles from André, then started down the road ahead of them at a pace which made it hard for them to keep up with him.

Fortunately it was downhill, and Tomás took them through dark, deserted streets where there was no-one to stare at the strange sight they must have made.

Sāona stumbled, and André, without speaking, picked her up in his arms and ran on.

Then the Quay was in sight and Tomás tore along it, shouting:

"*M'sieur* come! Wait! *M'sieur* here!"

It was difficult in the darkness to know who could be listening to him, but as André caught up with him, breathless from the speed at which he had run, he saw the Negro stop.

There, just below the edge of the Quay, was a rowing-boat in which there were four sailors.

"*M'sieur* here!" Tomás cried again, and one of the sailors said:

"About time! We were just leaving!"

He spoke Creole with a nasal accent, and although it was impossible in the darkness to see his face, André thought he must be a Negro.

He picked up Sāona in his arms and handed her to a sailor, who set her down in the boat.

Then he drew the gold louis he had ready in his pocket and pressed them into Tomás's hand.

"No, *M'sieur*, no!"

"Bless you, Tomás. I can never thank you enough," André said, and jumped into the boat before he could protest any further.

The sailors rowed away from the Quay and André looked back to see Tomás watching them go.

He waved his hand with a sigh of relief, and realised that the incredible good fortune that had befriended him ever since his arrival in Haiti had not failed him now.

He could see behind the town the outline of the high mountains against the stars, and he wondered if the Voodoo drums were telling those who might be interested that they had escaped.

Then he felt Sāona's fingers slip into his and he knew that she was feeling as he did, that it was all too wonderful to be true.

They came up against the side of a ship and André realised that it was a huge four-masted Schooner with the American flag flying at her stern.

They were helped aboard, then a man who he supposed was the Captain came towards them.

"I was informed, Sir," he said, "by the Officer who has just come from the shore in another boat, that you require a passage to America."

As he spoke, a sailor lifted a lantern to illuminate both André's face and the Captain's.

It was then that André realised that the Captain, on looking at him in the light, had stiffened.

Quite obviously he did not like what he saw.

Quickly, because he knew what was in the man's mind, André explained in English:

"I am *Comte* de Villaret and this lady is my wife. You will understand, Captain, that to reach here in safety it was necessary for us to be disguised, which included altering the colour of our skins."

"You're a Frenchman?" the Captain asked.

"I am a white man," André replied, "but you

know that had I been discovered, my life would not have been worth one cent."

He knew as he spoke that that was exactly what Jacques had said to him.

The Captain held out his hand.

"Welcome aboard, *Comte!*" he said. "I sure hope we can make you and the little lady comfortable."

"We will be very grateful to be under the protection of the flag of the United States of America," André replied.

"We can promise you that," the Captain replied. "Actually you're in luck, Sir, if I may say so."

André waited for the explanation and the Captain went on:

"We've just carried our Ambassador to Jamaica, and the cabin he and his wife occupied on the voyage is not only vacant but a real credit to this vessel."

"Thank you again," André said with a smile.

The Captain snapped his fingers.

"Mr. Marshberg," he said to an Officer standing near them, "escort the *Comte* and *Comtesse* below and see that they're looked after right and proper."

The young Officer, looking at them with curiosity, showed them to a large and comfortable cabin.

It contained a huge, old-fashioned box-bed which occupied one wall and had curtains that could be pulled across for privacy, or to make it less obvious as a piece of furniture during the day.

There were arm-chairs, a table, and a lantern hanging from the ceiling which lit the whole place with a golden light.

The Officer told them to ask if they needed anything, and a servant followed them into the cabin with the bundles which Tomás had thrown into the boat.

The door shut and André stood looking at Sãona with a smile on his lips.

He put out his arms, and would have pulled her to him, but she gave a little cry.

"No . . . no!" she said. "Not until I feel I am myself again!"

"Very well," he answered. "But it is certainly a

strange marriage where all the bride wants to do is
hide her face!"

"I want to look . . . lovely for you," Sāona said
quickly, "and not feel as I feel now."

"And what is that?" André asked.

He was opening one of the bundles as he spoke,
knowing where Tomás had put the bark of the tree
that would turn them white.

"I feel ugly, dusty, tired . . . and yet very, very
happy," Sāona said, as if she was choosing her words.

"If you say it like that," André said, "I shall kiss
you, whatever you think you look like."

"I want our kiss to be as wonderful as it was
when you kissed me in . . . the garden," she said.
"I never knew a kiss . . . would be like . . . reaching
Heaven."

It was hard not to touch her when she spoke to
him like that, but he pulled out a little packet of the
powdered bark from amongst his clothes.

As he did so, the leather bag containing the gold
louis fell out too and spilled all over the floor.

He laughed.

"I took a lot of precautions in case these bundles
were left behind by mistake," he said, "and now I
have to take all the diamonds out of my coat, where
I concealed them, and put them back in their bag."

Sāona gave a little cry.

"I had forgotten about them! You have them
safe?"

"I have them safe," André replied, "and I think
you will be glad of them, my precious, when we reach
America."

He left the louis lying on the floor as he put
some of the bark into a bowl that stood amongst the
other washing-things in a corner of the cabin.

He added the amount of water according to Tomás's instructions and stirred it until it was well mixed.

It looked, after a few seconds, as clear and inno-
cuous as it had done when Tomás had brought it to
them in the garden to wash their hands.

Sāona sat down in front of the mirror and pulled

first the dark veil from her head, then the wimple. Her golden hair fell over her shoulders.

André put the bowl down in front of her.

"This is what you want," he said. "I am not going to look at you while you transform yourself back into the little Saint with whom I fell in love in the woods."

"I am . . . not a Saint," Sāona answered. "I am . . . your wife . . . have you forgotten?"

"I have not forgotten," André replied. "And hurry, because I am anxious to treat you as a wife and not as a Mulatto Nun."

Sāona began to dab her face with the liquid, using a handkerchief.

"It stings a little," she said, "but the Reverend Mother gave me a special cream made with honey and rose-petals which she said would take away any irritation."

"I hope you will not use it all," André said. "Remember, I shall want some."

There was a knock on the door and he went to answer it.

"The Captain's compliments, Sir. He wondered if you'd like some supper and a bottle of wine. We're raising anchor."

"Please thank the Captain," André said, "and say that we are delighted to accept his suggestion."

He closed the door.

"Hurry," he said to Sāona, "and when I have made myself look presentable, we will dine in state and I shall be able to toast my wife on our wedding-night."

"I have nearly finished," Sāona replied. "I am thankful that the Reverend Mother thought it necessary to colour only my face and my hands."

André took off his coat and hung it up carefully so that the diamonds would not drop from inside the lining.

Tomorrow, he thought, he would slip them back into the bag in which they had been conveyed originally.

Tonight he was too tired.

At the same time, however tired he was, he knew that because it would please Sāona, he must remove the dye that Jacques had applied so skilfully to his body and which had served him well.

Sāona jumped up from the chair on which she had been sitting.

"Look!" she cried. "Now I am 'me,' and, I hope, the wife my husband wanted to marry."

André looked at her and his eyes held hers.

"In a very little while," he said, "I will tell you exactly what your husband feels about you. But first, as the dye stained me all over, I suggest you draw the curtains round the bed and rest before our dinner arrives."

Her eyes were very large in her face as she looked at him. Then she picked up her bundle.

André began to undo his cravat.

"If you take my advice," he said, "you will take off your clothes and put on a nightgown and a wrap, if you have one. After all, you are only dining with your husband, and he does not count!"

"I . . . I think it will . . . make me . . . shy," Sāona murmured.

"I like you shy," André replied. "And now I warn you, I am going to take off everything I have on!"

She gave a little cry and disappeared into the curtained bed.

André pulled off his clothes and started to apply the liquid in the same way that Sāona had done.

It was miraculous how quickly it removed what he had thought was a hard-and-fast dye.

First his face became white, then one side of his chest, and he was just starting on the other side when there was a knock on the door.

Quickly he fastened a towel round him before he said:

"Come in!"

A steward entered the cabin carrying a tray in his hands.

It was piled with dishes and there was also a bottle of wine in an ice-cooler.

He set it down on the table.

"Shall I stay and serve your meal, Sir?"

He looked at André as he spoke, and his mouth dropped open as he exclaimed:

"I sure never seed a piebald man aforel"

Realising that that might sound like a rather impertinent remark, he added:

"Beg pardon, Sir."

"That is all right," André replied. "And we would prefer to wait on ourselves, thank you very much."

The man scurried away and André wondered what sort of story he would relate to the rest of the ship's crew.

He finally removed nearly all the stain, dried himself, and, pulling a clean if rather creased shirt from his bundle, put it on.

There was, fortunately, a pair of comfortable long pantaloons, and when he was what he thought decently covered, he pulled back the curtains.

"Dinner is waiting, M'Lady!" he announced, then saw that Sãona was fast asleep.

She had, as he suggested, put on a nightgown, and her white wrapper was lying on the end of the bed.

Her head must have no sooner rested on the pillow than, from sheer exhaustion, she had dropped into a deep, dreamless slumber.

André stood looking down at her with a very tender expression on his face.

She looked unbelievably lovely, with her fair hair falling over the pillow and her skin even whiter than he remembered it, her eye-lashes dark against her cheeks.

She was very young, very innocent, he thought, with a kind of halo of purity that he had never known in any other woman.

Softly, he pulled the curtains together again.

Then he sat down, ate a little of the supper, and drank some of the wine.

He found that he was quite hungry, and he knew it was because he was no longer tense with fear and fleeing for his life and, more important, for Sāona's.

It was hard to realise now how terrifying the last two days had been.

He had known that Tomás was afraid that they would be captured before they reached Le Cap, and he had known too that it was quite likely when they entered the town that some officious soldier or newly appointed bureaucrat would insist on questioning them.

There were so many terrible things that might have happened, and yet, thanks to God and Damballah, they were safe, safe not only for the moment but for the rest of their lives.

André sat alone at the table, with a glass in his hand, thinking of the people he had met since he came to Haiti—of Jacques, Orchis, Tomás, the Reverend Mother, and most of all, Sāona.

She was what he had always wanted, what he had always longed for as a wife but thought it was unlikely he would ever find.

She was young, far younger than he had ever expected his wife to be, but he knew that she was old and wise in all the things that mattered.

She personified the ideals and principles which, hidden from a cynical world, had always been there deep in his soul.

The steward came and took the tray away and André realised that he had practically finished the whole bottle of wine himself.

Then, because he was exceedingly tired, he undressed and got into bed.

He looked for a long moment at the lovely face beside him on the next pillow, until with a little smile he decided that as they had all their lives in front of them, he could not be so cruel as to awaken her.

*   *   *

The ship was moving steadily through the calm water.

There was not much wind and the list to starboard was very slight, just enough to make anyone feel they were climbing either uphill or down as they moved about the cabin.

André opened his eyes.

There was a faint glow of light coming through the port-holes and he thought it must be still very early in the morning.

He looked through the curtains, which he had drawn back before he went to sleep, so as to get as much air as possible, and saw his wife sitting at the other end of the cabin, brushing her hair in front of the mirror.

She was wearing only her nightgown and he thought that she must have slipped very softly from the bed beside him so as not to awaken him.

He watched her for a long moment, seeing the light glint on her hair, the graceful movement of her arm, the slimness of her figure beneath the plain nightgown which must have been made by the Nuns.

She finished what she was doing, rose, and, walking carefully because of the list of the ship, went back towards the bed.

He watched her through half-closed eyes, knowing that she thought he was still asleep.

She reached the bed, climbed in very carefully, and lay down on her side, not touching him.

It was then that André turned over and put his arm across her to pull her closer to him.

"You are awake!" she exclaimed accusingly.

"I was watching someone very lovely making herself beautiful for me."

"Oh, André . . . I am so sorry," she cried. "I went to sleep last night . . . and only when I awoke this morning did I realise I had . . . missed my wedding-dinner."

"We will have many more dinners to make up for it," he said. "It was a very strange wedding-night, my lovely one, because my wife was not in the least interested in me!"

"You know that is . . . not true. I was just so . . . tired . . . so very tired . . . but I did not . . . mean to go to sleep."

"I was tired too, my darling," he said, "otherwise I might have been brutal enough to have awakened you."

"I . . . I wish you . . . had," she whispered.

He looked down at her, then turned her face, which she had hidden against his shoulder, up towards his.

"I am awake now," he said, "and so are you, my beautiful white bride."

"And you . . . are very handsome . . . my wonderful white . . . husband."

He pulled her suddenly, almost violently, against him.

"It is true," he said. "We are married! Do you realise, my darling, we are married?"

His lips took her captive and he kissed her at first violently, as if it relieved his feelings, then more gently. His mouth felt the sweetness of hers, and his hands touched her body in a way that made her tremble against him.

"I love you!" he said. "God, how I love you! And we have escaped! My precious, do you realise? We have escaped!"

"I was afraid," Sāona said, "so . . . afraid that either the soldiers would catch up with us, or when we reached Le Cap something would . . . happen and we would be . . . killed."

There was a note in her voice which told André that the horrors of what had happened when she was a child were never far from her mind.

Because he loved her, because her feelings were more important than his, he said very quietly:

"We are safe now, my darling. What we have to do is forget the past. It will not be easy, but I think that because we shall be so happy together, everything that is terrifying will recede and gradually vanish altogether."

"When I am . . . safe in your arms . . it is . . . easy to . . . forget."

"That is what I hoped," he said. "It is easy to remember also all the things we have enjoyed, and the people who have been kind to us, like the Reverend Mother, Tomás, and the Priest last night."

"At least . . . we are . . . married," Sāona said. "We are married?"

There was a sudden fear in her voice as if she thought it was either not legal or perhaps a dream.

"We are married," André said firmly, "but because I think it will make you happy, my precious, we will have a Service of Blessing either in a Catholic Church in America or when we get back to London."

"I am . . . happy as I . . . am," Sāona replied, "but I would like to . . . have looked beautiful for you on our wedding-day. I . . . hated that horrible brown stuff on my face."

"It was a very necessary precaution," André said. "If I had not stained my skin I might never have reached the Habitation de Villaret or found you."

"I love you!" Sāona whispered. "And I love the tree whose bark made you look like a Mulatto, though it is something you could never be inside."

André knew that the fear the Mulattos had aroused in her would perhaps be erasable, but where he was concerned, he would always remember the friendship that Jacques had given him.

He was determined that one day, perhaps through Kirk, he would pay Jacques back for his kindness.

Aloud he said:

"While we are being grateful, there is someone else we must never forget."

"Who is that?" Sāona asked.

"Damballah," he replied with a smile. "He protected us. If the drums had not warned Tomás, I might still have been in the house when the soldiers arrived."

Sāona gave a little cry.

"Oh, André . . . André! Suppose you had been . . . killed . . . I could never have . . . loved anybody else . . . I would just have grown old and died in the Convent . . . like those poor old Nuns."

"It did not happen," André said soothingly, "but we will always remember the drums gratefully."

He sighed, then he said:

"When I came to Haiti I never thought I would

believe in Voodoo. I thought the drums were something evil."

"To us they were . . . the drums of love!" Sāona
replied. "They saved you, and thanks to them we
are now married and safe on this wonderful ship."

"That is right, they were the drums of love,"
André agreed. "We will think of them with affection
for the rest of our lives."

He kissed her forehead as he spoke, then he felt
her lift her mouth to his, inviting his kiss.

"You are so lovely!" he said. "So perfect in every
way that even now I am afraid that you are a Saint,
whom I dare not touch."

"You . . . are touching . . . me," she said in a
breathless little voice.

"Not as closely as I want to do," André answered.
"I want to kiss and touch you until I am quite sure
that every little part of you belongs to me. Soon I will
kiss you, my darling, from your shining hair to the
soles of your little feet."

"I . . . would . . . like that," Sāona whispered.

"But at the moment," André said, "I find it hard
to do anything but kiss your lips and touch the softness of your skin."

He kissed her eyes, then her neck, and felt her
quiver.

Then gently, so as not to frighten her, he pulled
the plain nightgown from her shoulders so that he
could kiss her breasts.

He was very gentle, very tender, exploring her
as if she were a flower, the lily that was symbolic of
her beauty and her purity.

Then, as he felt her body quiver against his, as
he knew her heart was beating as frantically as his,
his lips became more possessive, more insistent.

He knew, as he felt a flicker of fire run through
her, that she wanted him as he wanted her.

"I . . . love . . . you," she murmured.

"And I adore you. Do I make you happy?"

"You make . . . me excited. . . ."

"What do you feel?"

THE DRUMS OF LOVE 161

"Little thrills . . . running up and . . . down my spine. . . ."

"Thrills?"

"They are little . . . tongues of fire . . . in my body. . . ."

"I can feel them on your lips."

"Kiss me . . . oh, André . . . kiss me."

Somewhere far away in the back of his mind, as he kissed her, André thought that the gods who had given them to each other would understand and be glad.

Man could not live without love, and it was a reflection of the love which came from the Divine.

It seemed to André in that moment that the God of the Christians, of the Buddhists, of the Muslims, and of Voodoo were all one.

They all inspired man to seek beyond himself, telling him that the only way of life was not through hatred and evil but love.

What he felt for Sãona was, he knew, all that was best and highest within himself.

The love that she gave him came from a heart that beat in unison with his and from a soul that was filled with a purity and beauty that came from Heaven.

"I love you, I love you!" he murmured. "I worship you, my darling, my little Saint, my wife!"

"Hold me . . . closer . . . oh, André . . . I love you . . . so much . . . it is frightening. . ."

"Nothing will ever frighten you again, my precious."

"My love for you frightens me . . . it is so big and . . . becoming bigger. . . ."

"I will make you love me a thousand times more than you do now—I will fill your life and mine with love."

"Darling . . . darling . . . I . . . love . . . you."

Her breath was coming gaspingly between her parted lips, and there was the glimmer of the first awakening of desire in her eyes.

She looked so beautiful that André could only murmur:

"My lovely—my beautiful, perfect little wife."

His words were lost in the overflowing of happiness within his heart and the feeling that he had had in the garden, that they were no longer in the world but flying higher and higher up towards the sun.

"I . . . adore . . . you!" Sāona whispered against his lips. "Love me . . . oh, André, love . . . me."

Then they were no longer two people but one, not only in this life but for all eternity.

ABOUT THE AUTHOR

BARBARA CARTLAND, the world's most famous romantic novelist, who is also an historian, playwright, lecturer, political speaker and television personality, has now written over 200 books. She has also had many historical works published and has written four autobiographies as well as the biographies of her mother and that of her brother Ronald Cartland, who was the first Member of Parliament to be killed in the last war. This book has a preface by Sir Winston Churchill. Barbara Cartland has sold 80 million books over the world, more than half of these in the U.S.A. She broke the world record in 1975 by writing twenty books, and her own record in 1976 with twenty-one. In private life, Barbara Cartland, who is a Dame of the Order of St. John of Jerusalem, has fought for better conditions and salaries for Midwives and Nurses. As President of the Royal College of Midwives (Hertfordshire Branch), she has been invested with the first Badge of Office ever given in Great Britain, which was subscribed to by the Midwives themselves. She has also championed-the-cause for old people and founded the first Romany Gypsy Camp in the world. Barbara Cartland is deeply interested in Vitamin Therapy and is President of the British National Association for Health.

BARBARA CARTLAND
PRESENTS
THE ANCIENT WISDOM SERIES

The world's all-time bestselling author of romantic fiction, Barbara Cartland, has established herself as High Priestess of Love in its purest and most traditionally romantic form.

"We have," she says, "in the last few years thrown out the spiritual aspect of love and concentrated only on the crudest and most debased sexual side.

"Love at its highest has inspired mankind since the beginning of time. Civilization's greatest pictures, music, prose and poetry have all been written under the influence of love. This love is what we all seek despite the temptations of the sensuous, the erotic, the violent and the perversions of pornography.

"I believe that for the young and the idealistic, my novels with their pure heroines and high ideals are a guide to happiness. Only by seeking the Divine Spark which exists in every human being, can we create a future built on the foundation of faith."

Barbara Cartland is also well known for her Library of Love, classic tales of romance, written by famous authors like Elinor Glyn and Ethel M. Dell, which have been personally selected and specially adapted for today's readers by Miss Cartland.

"These novels I have selected and edited for my 'Library of Love' are all stories with which the readers can identify themselves and also be assured that right will triumph in the end. These tales elevate and activate the mind rather than debase it as so many modern stories do."

Now, in August, Bantam presents the first four novels in a new Barbara Cartland Ancient Wisdom series. The books are THE FORBIDDEN CITY by Barbara Cartland, herself; THE ROMANCE OF TWO WORLDS by Marie Corelli; THE HOUSE OF FULFILLMENT by L. Adams Beck; and BLACK LIGHT by Talbot Mundy.

"Now I am introducing something which I think is of vital importance at this moment in history. Following my own autobiographical book I SEEK THE MIRACULOUS, which Dutton is publishing in hardcover this summer, I am offering those who seek 'the world behind the world' novels which contain, besides a fascinating story, the teaching of Ancient Wisdom.

"In the snow-covered vastnesses of the Himalayas, there are lamaseries filled with manuscripts which have been kept secret for century upon century. In the depths of the tropical jungles and the arid wastes of the deserts, there are also those who know the esoteric mysteries which few can understand.

"Yet some of their precious and sacred knowledge has been revealed to writers in the past. These books I have collected, edited and offer them to those who want to look beyond this greedy, grasping, materialistic world to find their own souls.

"I believe that Love, human and divine, is the jail-breaker of that prison of selfhood which confines and confuses us . . .

"I believe that for those who have attained enlightenment, super-normal (not super-human) powers are available to those who seek them."

All Barbara Cartland's own novels and her Library of Love are available in Bantam Books, wherever paperbacks are sold. Look for her Ancient Wisdom Series to be available in August.

Barbara Cartland's Library of Love

The World's Great Stories of Romance Specially Abridged by Barbara Cartland For Today's Readers.

☐	11487	**THE SEQUENCE** by Elinor Glyn	$1.50
☐	11468	**THE BROAD HIGHWAY** by Jeffrey Farnol	$1.50
☐	10927	**THE WAY OF AN EAGLE** by Ethel M. Dell	$1.50
☐	10926	**THE REASON WHY** by Elinor Glyn	$1.50
☐	10527	**THE KNAVE OF DIAMONDS** by Ethel M. Dell	$1.50
☐	10506	**A SAFETY MATCH** by Ian Hay	$1.50
☐	11465	**GREATHEART** by Ethel M. Dell	$1.50
☐	11048	**THE VICISSITUDES OF EVANGELINE** by Elinor Glyn	$1.50 $1.50
☐	11369	**THE BARS OF IRON** by Ethel M. Dell	$1.50
☐	11370	**MAN AND MAID** by Elinor Glyn	$1.50
☐	11391	**THE SONS OF THE SHEIK** by E. M. Hull	$1.50
☐	11376	**SIX DAYS** by Elinor Glyn	$1.50
☐	11467	**THE GREAT MOMENT** by Elinor Glyn	$1.50
☐	11560	**CHARLES REX** by Ethel M. Dell	$1.50
☐	11816	**THE PRICE OF THINGS** by Elinor Glyn	$1.50
☐	11821	**TETHERSTONES** by Ethel M. Dell	$1.50

Buy them at your local bookstore or use this handy coupon for ordering:

Barbara Cartland

The world's bestselling author of romantic fiction.
Her stories are always captivating tales of intrigue,
adventure and love.

☐	2993	NEVER LAUGH AT LOVE	$1.25
☐	02972	A DREAM FROM THE NIGHT	$1.25
☐	02987	CONQUERED BY LOVE	$1.25
☐	10337	HUNGRY FOR LOVE	$1.25
☐	2917	DREAM AND THE GLORY	$1.50
☐	10971	THE RHAPSODY OF LOVE	$1.50
☐	10715	THE MARQUIS WHO HATED WOMEN	$1.50
☐	10972	LOOK, LISTEN AND LOVE	$1.50
☐	10975	A DUEL WITH DESTINY	$1.50
☐	10976	CURSE OF THE CLAN	$1.50
☐	10977	PUNISHMENT OF A VIXEN	$1.50
☐	11101	THE OUTRAGEOUS LADY	$1.50
☐	11168	A TOUCH OF LOVE	$1.50
☐	11169	THE DRAGON AND THE PEARL	$1.50

Barbara Cartland

The world's bestselling author of romantic fiction.
Her stories are always captivating tales of intrigue,
adventure and love.

☐	11372	LOVE AND THE LOATHSOME LEOPARD	$1.50
☐	11410	THE NAKED BATTLE	$1.50
☐	11512	THE HELL-CAT AND THE KING	$1.50
☐	11537	NO ESCAPE FROM LOVE	$1.50
☐	11580	THE CASTLE MADE FOR LOVE	$1.50
☐	11579	THE SIGN OF LOVE	$1.50
☐	11595	THE SAINT AND THE SINNER	$1.50
☐	11649	A FUGITIVE FROM LOVE	$1.50
☐	11797	THE TWISTS AND TURNS OF LOVE	$1.50
☐	11801	THE PROBLEMS OF LOVE	$1.50
☐	11751	LOVE LEAVES AT MIDNIGHT	$1.50
☐	11882	MAGIC OR MIRAGE	$1.50
☐	10712	LOVE LOCKED IN	$1.50
☐	11959	LORD RAVENSCAR'S REVENGE	$1.50
☐	11488	THE WILD, UNWILLING WIFE	$1.50
☐	11555	LOVE, LORDS, AND LADY-BIRDS	$1.50

Buy them at your local bookstore or use this handy coupon: